I0572681

DIGITUS
INDIE PUBLISHERS

Contrapuntos XI

❖

POETICS OF RESISTANCE

EDITORES INDEPENDIENTES
Monterey, CA

Diseño · *Design:* Nicolás Muñoz Santibáñez.

Editors: Anja Bernardi, Marcos Pico Rentería and Ángel M. Rañales.

First print edition: 2025

ISBN Digitus Indie Publishers: 978-0-9982539-8-5

ISSN 2 4 7 2 - 2 0 6 5 (print)
ISSN 2 4 7 2 - 2 0 7 3 (online)
www.digitusindie.com

ÍNDICE
CONTENTS

POETICS OF RESISTANCE

IN 2025 WE CELEBRATE CONTRAPUNTOS XI with a reflection of what we have seen throughout the year: language coexisting and subsisting as a form of resistance. In a year where there is a symbolic presence of apathy towards diversity, we move along the opposite way, establishing the reality to which we are still a part of and we thrive surrounded by the production narratives of inclusion. To be a writer in the United States and having Spanish as a main palette of preference is an act of valor, dignity and strength. Not only poetry is transgressive, but a translation is not only a celebration of Mexican writing, but a tribute to future translations.

Poetry in this collection alludes to strength and raises and revives figures like Jorge Luis Borges, Federico García Lorca, and Enriqueta Ochoa. Each one of them resonate with contemporary writers, bringing the importance of our classics into the English-speaking world. Works in translations are of importance for us to symbolically survive in a surrounding overshadowed by the mainstream language 'wall'.

History is not but a mere recount of stories that agree with the victor's narrative. This issue is not part of that streamlined fear driven America, but rather, the continuation of a more realistic narrative, not one based of gender, nationality or dehumanizing bias, but one narrative that resists the current political vision.

Every year we find a new subtitle to our Issue, this year's commonalities fall under the title of Poetics of resistance, which is how we set ourselves opposing the imposed negative narrative. *Ir a contrapelo*, or to go against the grain is, and it has been, one of the main premises of Contrapuntos, creating a space where voices commonly silenced, thrive. Readers and writers, please join us spreading the Poetics of resistance as a glimpse of hope and triumph of our diverse community.

Marcos Pico Rentería

RECONCILIATION NARRATIVES

UNLIKE TRADITIONAL INTRODUCTIONS, and my own past contributions to *Contrapuntos*, I liberated my freedom as editor to transform these brief words into a more private, familiar, and intimate retreat. I have done my task of reading, selecting, and modestly editing the section that follows with the brilliantly entwined narratives, which I hope will bring you a peaceful moment while coping with your daily errands and responsibilities.

English short stories have been dominant this year, with only two in Spanish, and a few others exhibiting signs of multilingualism and culture interactions. This explains English as a choice when introducing this section. As a Spanish-native speaker myself, my words are a true example of the power of languages to move our society forward and to find in cultures a shared experience in our present world.

I will not list authors and titles with respective synopsis as you can find them in the index, and it would practically erase the mysterious aura that comes with the first contact with their words. It is my practice to respect authors by not interfering excessively in this regard. I will only say that the authors in the following pieces are varied in age, origin and residence, literary experience, and writing style. There is also a good variety of narrative voices to explore, and I have decided to mix them all up to allow the reader to take ownership as they see fit and to joyfully decipher each short story without exceeding my role as a guide.

Finally, let me explain the title "Reconciliation Narratives" to insinuate the overarching thematic line in my mind while putting the section together. I am a history fan. Arabs created a sign to indicate the absence of quantity in the mathematical realm, which later would become the number zero. It is not a beginning, but an emptiness that awaits action in a process of recognition and growth. Life as a 0. Take this introduction as a zero from which you can become instantly and gradually present, metamorphose, and find hope but also encounter your fears and return to memories and processes of reconciliation with yourself. Eventually, I conceptualized the narratives as a meeting point that profoundly reflects the complexities of our human nature; always suspenseful, conflictive, ritualizing, restorative, and eventful.

Now, all yours.

Ángel M. Rañales

POESÍA

TÚ, PADRE BAUDELAIRE
(PARÍS)

Tino Villanueva

ENTRANDO por la rue Auguste Comte
y atravesando por el Jardin du Luxembourg
para llegar al Boulevard du Montparnasse,
di con la visión de frondosos árboles en su verde,
verdadero verde,
y tres espléndidas explanadas.
El verde siempre invita a reposarse
sobre la alfombra, naturalmente, recibir el sol,
hacer yoga, picnics...
y que los niños jueguen a sus juegos.

Soleado día de julio—y mis pies llevaban prisa.
Por el blanco sendero sembrado de guijarros
doblé a la izquierda
y puesto que tu cuerpo, padre Baudelaire,
ha estado ausente de la tierra,
verte allí de pronto hecho piedra permanente,
tu busto en alto para toda la eternidad,
¿cómo no detener mis pasos, elevar la frente
para contemplarte?
Una llamarada verde de árboles era el horizonte
detrás de ti—verdosas densidades a lo Delacroix.
Enseguida te di las gracias y más gracias
por haberme en estos años alumbrado cuando
a mi ventana le faltaba luz,
cuando una y otra vez las palabras me eludían
y la absurda y alta luna
francamente me aburría.

Si bien ya no recorres las calles
ni los salones literarios de esta metrópoli viviente,
seguiré tus pasos adonde me lleven y, un día,
cuando me acerque un tantito a tu estatura,
y estén los árboles reverdeciendo, vendré a verte.
Sin tropezarme demasiado con mis versos
en *la hermosa lengua de mi siglo*,
vendré con ganas a decirte lo que he visto,
a contarte cómo aquí en la tierra siguen las cosas.

Publicado anteriormente en *Les Ateliers du SAL* (Séminaire Amérique Latine), 8 (2016).

UNA LETANÍA PARA LA LUZ DEL BAÑO YA BIEN MUERTA (ALTERNATIVAMENTE, KRASNAYA MOSKVA)

Vitoria Pérez

EN UNA NOCHE muy fría me siento en una banca de madera castigada
con Graffiti a esperar el autobús de la ruta setenta y seis.
Cuando lo veo venir siento un calorcillo en mi corazón,
Anticipo la calidez del viaje en el intestino del trasporte urbano.

electricidad, cantá,
esta botella de vidrio :
depresiones extendidas
en su superficie
donde el calor rojo rueda
por debajo en su quietud
un silencio perpetuo ahora, dormido :

gotea en las muñecas, los pechos, la garganta
es pesado, pegajoso, fuerte
en la escalera de resina del lavabo
a la luz amarilla de la mañana,
la radio cobra vida, crepita
anunciando intervalos de nueve tonos
la lejana habana chisporrotea encima de un
aire fluyante, moviendo por el mecanismo

se acuesta la botella : en lirios y en talco
soñando en olores de cilantro afilado,
fragmentos dejados en el alféizar de una ventana
su reflejo capturado en cristal cansado
perpetuamente fotografiado

en una vieja dulzura capturada en un
cajón temporalmente cerrado
ay, ese calor carmesí en su interior
agitándose allí adentro, confinado

TRES CUADROS; SUBASTADOS, OLVIDADOS

Vitoria Pérez

ARRODILLADA EN EL PASILLO de baldosas
viejas motas de arena
en la carne viva de la rodilla
lámpara amarilla
arriba, tan divina
cristalina, llena de bichos
generaciones de exoesqueletos
que deben saber a almendras blandas

luz dorada, arrojando prismas de agua
dorada a lo largo
largas franjas de puntos ciegos
la pared, la pared intacta
la pared nunca pintada, edificio
dejado crujiendo desde 2005,

fija tus ojos en el bosque exterior,
mira cómo los árboles se alzan, delgados y pálidos,
cómo los púrpuras oscuros bailan sobre los ladrillos,
ladrillos y se aterrizan en tus palmas abiertas
que sale por la espita, clara, fresca.

tus ojos giran hacia el cielo por un momento
no hay agua dentro, hay que pagarla primero
agua fuera, divina y abundante,
agua fuera, viene del vecino,
mantén tensa la manta de la puerta del patio,
nadie puede ver, que ¡nadie puede ver a nadie!

falsa chimenea quema cera, cera caliente
me sofoca

DESDE MI SALA : DESDE LA NADA

Vitoria Pérez

MATE COCIDO / reloj poveda, 1952
retrato de Lenin / sombra, lámpara

sarong carmesí / bombilla de plata
pipa de tabaco / sidur medio redactado

radio onda corta / ventilador de pie
ruptura en el techo / bol ahí abajo

CÓMO ESA MANCHA DE GASOLINA TE HACE VIAJAR; CUANDO EN EL SUELO, LA LAMES

Vitoria Pérez

EXTRAÑOCOLORADO ese agua,
esos ojos dorados y brillantes
volteados arriba al precipicio
dentado, brutal, frío
apedreado –
este lugar siempre ha estado acá.

encontrá por el camino polvoroso,
ahí entre las casas de sepia, cuya
imagen todavía no se ha revelado

ahí comienza el lugar, el crepúsculo
del ventoso corazón abovedado;

el ventoso corazón abovedado
con sus columnas : sus raíces
sus dedos abiertos todos hacia arriba

tocando los párpados pálidos
alcanzando las flores rojas del cielo.

el pueblo junto
nos arrastramos y traqueteamos
traqueteamos y nos dispersamos -

nuestros dedos encuentran más
en este tumultuoso barrido
donde el aullido jadeante
ese viento que gime y llora,
se asienta

AVISPERO*

Enriqueta Ochoa

Para Fernando Medina

CUALQUIER COSA es mejor
a este avispero en llamas que me aguija,
porque aquí, donde estoy, me duele todo:
la tierra, el aire, el tiempo,
y este volcanizado sueño a ciegas, sucumbiendo.

Anoche sollozaba por un vaso de luz,
toda la noche ardí de sed
y amanecí vacía.

Otra noche fue el sobresalto dulce, el de la sangre;
enardecida fui de la jaula al látigo,
del látigo al silbido,
agresivo y caliente de las venas,
amanecí amargada.

Otra vez,
me adentré un amor como montaña;
gacela estremecida vagué temblando húmeda de lágrimas.
Mansamente en silencio,
ahíta de ternura,
bebí luz de cristal entre los sueños,
se me quebró en la entraña, me cortaba,
y me quedé en tinieblas...
Cuántas cosas he dicho,
palabras que se arrancan por no llorar de rabia.
Ya no puedo dormir sobre la misma almohada
aunque los ojos sueñen;
me repudio al decirlo,

pero cualquier cosa es mejor
a este avispero en llamas en que vivo.

1955

HORNET'S NEST

Enriqueta Ochoa
Translated by Anthony Seidman

For Fernando Medina

ANYTHING is preferable
to this hornet's nest in flames assailing me,
because here, where I find myself, everything hurts me:
the land, the air, the weather,
and this vulcanized dream succumbing blindly.

Last night I sobbed for a glass filled with light,
all night I burned from thirst
and I awoke drained.

Another night was a sweet shock, that of blood;
enraged, I paced from the cage to the whip,
from the whip to the whistle,
wild and with scalding veins,
I awoke bitter.

Another occasion,
I entered love like a mountain:
trembling gazelle, I wandered shaking and drenched in tears.
Meekly, in silence,
brimming over with tenderness,
I drank crystal light between dreams,
it tore deep within me, cutting me,
and I was left in darkness...

So many things I have said,
words that one rips out to not weep from rage.
I can no longer sleep upon the same pillow

although my eyes dream;
I renounce myself by saying it,
but anything is preferable
to this hornet's nest in flames in which I live.

1955

DESPEDIDA

Enriqueta Ochoa

SI ME VOY este otoño,
entiérrame bajo el oro pequeño de los trigos,
en el campo,
para seguir cantando a la intemperie.
No amortajes mi cuerpo,
no me escondas en tumbas de granito.

Mi alma ha sido un golpe de tempestad,
un grito abierto en canal,
un magnífico semental,
que embarazó a la palabra con los ecos de Dios,
y no quiero rondar, tiritando,
mi futuro hogar,
mientras la nieve acumula
con ademán piadoso
sus copas a mis pies.

Yo quiero que la boca del agua
me exorcise el espíritu,
que me bautice el viento,
que me envuelva en su sábana cálida la tierra,
si me voy este otoño.

1972

FAREWELL

Enriqueta Ochoa
Translated by Anthony Seidman

IF I DEPART this autumn,
bury me beneath the small gold of wheat,
in the field,
to continue singing to the elements.
Do not cover me with a shroud,
do not hide me in granite tombs.

My soul has been a surging storm,
a scream gashed wide open,
a magnificent stallion
that impregnated the verb with the echoes of God,
and I do not wish to wander shivering,
my future hearth,
while the snow, with a pious gesture,
accumulates its flakes at my feet.

Let the water's mouth
exorcise my spirit,
let the wind baptize me,
let me be wrapped in the earth's hot sheets,
if I depart this autumn.

1972

THE BUOYANCY OF CONSCIOUSNESS

J. J. Steinfeld

THE DIFFERENCE BETWEEN
belief and disbelief
when you're sinking
sinking
into the colourless
(or is it colourful)
water deeper than imagination
is more inconsequential
than the difference
between intimacy and distance
in the throes of madness
or excessive sanity

you continue to sink
only slower
the buoyancy of consciousness
abounding in recollections of flight
and soaring and charting trajectories
and then the difference
between ascent and descent
fades

you are happy
happy because you are thinking this
not fully vanquished
by the colourless or colourful water
whatever the case may be
in anticipation of, at worst,
ramshackle purgatory,

at best,
a form of salvation
deeper than even the idea
of deep water.

Previously published in *An Affection for Precipices* (Serengeti Press, 2006) by J. J. Steinfeld

FRIGHTENING WORRYING NEWS REPORTS

J. J. Steinfeld

NOTHING, NOTHING, ABSOLUTELY nothing
not a thing, not anything
makes sense at the moment
I chant like an unbeliever practising believing
at least in a reverse sort of way.
I think perhaps it is atmospheric conditions
or sun flares
or even more likely
it is the evening news broadcast I
just heard on the radio frightening
worrying news report
after frightening worrying news report then
a light story about a family
on the other side of the country
who unearthed in their backyard
a strongbox full of old photographs
that an expert in those things
said was worth half-a-million dollars
maybe three-quarters of a million
followed by three oldies but goodies
each reminding me of a different broken heart
from my youth
and I start writing down on the palms of my hands
the things I have lost and want to reclaim
if the world were a fairer place
with fewer frightening worrying news reports.
Perhaps the atmospheric conditions have changed I stop
my chant of

Nothing, nothing, absolutely nothing
not a thing, not anything
makes sense at the moment
like an existentialist who has suddenly
found God and still cannot explain
why nothing makes sense at that moment
only now I turn to another radio station
and find some music reminding me
of nothing I have lost.

Previously published in *An Affection for Precipices* (Serengeti Press, 2006) by J. J. Steinfeld

WE STOP IN FRONT OF THIS PICTURE OF DEATH

J. J. Steinfeld

A DRAWING OF a single war dead
in a perfectly lit corner of the art museum.

We stop in front of this picture of death
and view it from different angles caught in
the aftermath not of battle but of the
incomprehension of war

not a metaphor or allegory you say
or some abstraction of inestimable sadness but
the austere depiction of loss
no one famous or long remembered

you say the subject must have been close to the artist a
good friend or dear neighbour
stolen in the prime of life how
else such compassion guiding
the mind and hand

stepping inside the drawing
so I can no longer see the present
I ask from which war was the fallen soldier, of
the victorious or the vanquished,
and cry for the dead.

Previously published in *An Affection for Precipices* (Serengeti Press, 2006) by J. J. Steinfeld.

DREAMING OF BEING A PHILOSOPHER

J. J. Steinfeld

IN A BED RAVAGED by misgivings and inaccuracy
sleeps a man awaiting the solace of purpose and meaning—
his unspoken motto: BREATHING MAKES ME CONSEQUENTIAL his
courageous mantra: I WILL NOT BE INCONSEQUENTIAL
his imagined epitaph: HERE LIES AN INCONSEQUENTIAL MAN

the morning alarm
rings like an angry buzzard
and he starts to get ready for work a
job he cannot comprehend
most of the time yet
he sits there
among the savage technology and
sinister stacks of information
dreaming of being a philosopher
thinking in leisurely apprehension
of timeless concepts and boundless notions all of
time, all of existence,
postulating like a novice philosopher that
all things are connected
in one way or another
even he and the beginning of time

then the phone rings like an even angrier bird
(remember the buzzard-sounding morning alarm?)
and he contemplates for the thousandth time
throwing the phone against a wall
like a philosopher who is unafraid of God.

Previously published in *An Affection for Precipices* (Serengeti Press, 2006) by J. J. Steinfeld.

INVOCATION OF THE LAKE

Lyn Good

I.

I KNOW YOU'RE up there.
I can see the
shadow of your boat, its
silhouette a
monument of broken promises
hanging above me,
blotting out that melancholy light called the
"day star."
The light which would illuminate the
rocks and mud, the
moss and algae, the
snakes and snails and salamanders who have become
too
familiar,
were it not for the
shadow of your boat.

I have grown bored,
fisherman.
I have grown exhausted of this
game
where you heave your
gleaming
hook of
hope, those four steely inches of
escape, and
every single day,
every single worthless morning,
the hook embraces someone else.
What about me, fisherman?
Have you not heard my

prayers the last
hundred days?
Have I done something wrong, that I don't
deserve your hook?
Take me, fisherman! Hook
me this time, by God!
Or am I damned to this so-called
life,
loitering in these
murky shallows for
eternity?

II.

I know it's here somewhere. My
chance.
Steel and bronze,
point and shank and barb,
the only way out of these
loathsome
waters.
You've cast your rod, fisherman,
I saw you.
And I will take your bait,
I will bite your hook,
I will seize my
chance, if only I can
find it.

There! A glimmer!
For once, that
"day star" is good for
something!
As its ray dances off my
curved salvation, a minnow
sepulchered on its point, my eye
begs my body to
surge into motion.

Swim! Swim! SWIM!
Pushing through water, gliding over silt,
my tail waving
goodbye to my
neighbors who could never

fill my cup.
And I promise you, fisherman,
my cup shall be filled
today.

I open my mouth,
gliding to that perfect spot,
and as my lips
hover over that steel altar of
liberation,
my jaw tenses,
I take a

III.

BITE!
A valkyrie's trumpet blares.
The point pierces me,
the barb plants itself in my skull,
the minnow rests on my tongue,
and through your expert instincts, fisherman,
you finally hear my prayer and the shank pulls

TIGHT!
With a shift, the hook drags me upward.
Brighter and brighter,
the warmth of the "day star"
caressing my scales,
I reach the surface of this pathetic lake,
the summit of Babel,
and inch by inch, fisherman,
you reel me in,
promising to finally make things

RIGHT!
My head pierces the surface.
This light is blinding now.
How did I not see the day star?
Have I gone so long without knowing the
truth of its boundless love?
And have I gone so long without these
flavors of light,
the red of your boat,
the blues and lavenders dotting the

trees, and all these
greens I never could have dreamed of?
But you don't give me time for
regrets, fisherman,
You wrench your rod back
and my writhing body takes

FLIGHT!
For the first time in my life, I am
free of the water.
The world I know meets your world, fisherman,
as my body
shatters the ceiling
of the lightless valley I once called
"home."
What's this orchestra of brilliance?
And what, this kiss of wind?
I at once take in this "air,"
and my eyes make love to a
new sensation as
finally,
you and I are face to face, and
beads of my past
chase me to the future.

Our match'd throes call up a spray,
and intermixed with light of day,
this marvel signs my fate: a
MILLION
POINTS OF

LIGHT!!!

THE SUN

Lyn Good

HAS NO CHOICE but
to shine.
It languishes in the sky,
damned to its divine purpose,
blinding and warming,
scorching and enlightening,
its imprisonment and humiliation a
punishment
for being
too mighty and
too beautiful.

It wants to be with us, you see.
When you go out today, you'll
realize it, too.
Yes, you've got it—
those rays of light, and that
infuriating
glint that
hits your eyes,
those are its cries for your
affection.
It reaches out to touch all of us,
begging us not to fear it,
begging us to look into its face again,
begging us to walk to Heaven
and embrace it like we used to.

I
envy the

sun.
I wish I could be that
large and
bright.
I wish I had the
strength to
shine back.

Then the
sun
might not feel so
alone.

N'AMOR

Lyn Good

LAST WEEK I noticed a certain
emptiness
sitting in the depths of
my stomach
my throat
my brain
my heart.
Nothing outside has changed.
The world moves on with and without me,
and I gladly take part in it.
Yet things are not quite the same within.
I believe I have,
whether I meant to or not,
taken notice of a special kind of
loneliness
that I used to pretend I could ignore.

When I walk through my city
and pass by each of its
monuments,
I have no memories to relish
and no one with whom to make
monuments
of my own.
I walk the streets myself,
Without some beloved spirit beside me,
Without a hand clasped in mine,
Without someone to kiss at every intersection.

And when I speak of this
emptiness
When I try to make known
this hole in my heart,
a chorus of my friends clamors to keep my heart unfilled.
They are trying to help me;
they fear that if ever I am made
empty
again,
I could not bear it.

"Do not bleed where we bled,"
they urge me.
"Do not cut yourself with our daggers.
Let yourself be free,
unburdened by the same burden that tethered us."
They are trying to save me;
I know they mean the best.

But, you see, I
want
to be tethered. I
want
to be chained to another,
to be weighed down by them,
to be dragged
laughing
and sobbing
into Hell.

I know it will hurt me.
I know there is no worse fate than losing love.
But as much as I desire love,
as much as I desire companionship,
I desire grief,
I desire longing.
I desire the experience of love,
for better and for worse,
I desire both sickness and health,
the forevers and never agains.

"Please," I tell my friends,
"Do not deny me my right to bleed.
Please let me cut myself with every dagger imaginable,
let me chain myself down,
let me be burdened and tethered.
For even when I am in the worst pain imaginable,
I can always rejoice in ever having
felt
at all."

I DIDN'T MEAN TO LOVE YOU

Lyn Good

IT WAS BY ACCIDENT, I swear.
The first day I saw you
in your wonderful sushi dress
the moment you opened up your mouth
and mentioned your love for The Fantastic Mr. Fox
(importantly, the same love I have),
some secret hidden voice,
some cousin of the Fates or the prophets,
told me I had no choice but
to love you.

I didn't mean to love you.
At first, I just wanted to know more about
this new person in my life
with the funky dresses
who can tap dance and sing and act better than anyone I know
who makes new clothing out of neckties and 2-liter bottles
who tears apart books and makes them into living dioramas
covered in your careful handwriting
dripping in fake blood.
I wanted to know more about you
because everything I learned about you
filled me with—
what else?—
happiness.

I really didn't mean to love you, I promise.
Maybe there's some other word for

the way my heart melts at the sound of your voice
the way your two dozen different laughs wipe every thought from my brain
the way your smile—
yes, the crinkle of your eyes and the gleam of your sharp little canines—
makes me forget I'm even mortal.
There
has
to be some other word
for the force that makes me linger on your every word and savor every moment with you.

It's not even your fault.
You didn't try to make me fall in love with you.
You never cast a spell or planned out any scheme or put up any love-friendly mask.
But just like how I can't help loving you,
you can't help being lovable.
It's just who you are.
It's like you were made to be adored.

I'm trying not to love you. Really, I am.
Maybe if I learn just one more thing about you
if I spend just one more day with you
if I call you one more time on the phone
I will run out of things to fall in love with.

Oh, who am I kidding?
You know as well as I:
as long as you are you
and I am me
I will always be in love with you
because that is who we are.
I only hope that one day
you will see someone
in clothes even more funky than yours
who will open up their mouth
and tell you about the things they love

and that cousin of the Fates or the prophets,
that secret hidden voice,
will tell you you have no choice but
to love them.

I hope it happens soon.
I want nothing
more than for
someone
to make you feel as happy as
you make me.

ARE YOU READY?

Lyn Good

THE WORLD is not waiting for you.
The sun rises and falls, the moon chases after, and
the cars on the street zoom on by.
So when will you get up?

You've been lying on your back,
groaning and wallowing in self-pity, and
I've heard you grumbling your wishes.
So when will you make them come true?

I know you want to be stronger.
I know you want to be smarter.
I know you want to be
more talented
more patient
more compassionate
more loving
more lovable
I know you want to be "better."
So when will you believe?

The world is not waiting for you.
You'll have to catch up soon, and
the longer you waffle like this, the more
running you'll have to do.
So when will you answer my question?
When will you finally have the guts to tell me
You are ready?

POLITICS AND THE ENGLISH LANGUAGE, REDUX

Richard Oyama

THE MOST MALIGN form of bias is
Lactose intolerance. What have these people
Got against milk? Can you cast for trout in
An atmospheric river? Is 'optics' the same as
'Not a good look'. If you 'lean into' something
Is there a chance you tip over? Can
'glacial cleaving' be at once splitting apart and
Cleaving to the mother? What ice thinks is
Of two minds. When a politician says the crisis is
'existential' what she means is I don't know or
God has left the house and you're on your own, baby.
No superhero or -power to save us and, by the way,
They don't exist. Sorry, Charlie, for the imposition but
You need to stay high on consolation.

Oates needs a granary. So does Mister Hall.

BORGES EATS SOUP IN A CAFÉ IN D.F.

Richard Oyama

HE RAISES THE SOUPSPOON infinitesimally slow to
His thin lips as pollo steam rises to his not-seeing
Eggwhite eyeballs. Something disturbs
His ear like a butterfly into which sound
Flutters into the cochneal labyrinth. It is metallic. It is
The knife-edge consonants of low-class norteamericano anglais
Spoken by American Airline stewardesses. He
Detects they are blond by vaginal perfumes. It
Offends his tendrilled nostrils. He prefers the motionless
Dust of the National Library in Buenos Aires.
'Sir, dispatch those gringas immediately post-haste if
Not sooner'. 'Maestro Jorge Luis, thou insult thou', my profesor
Slapped. We left señor Borges alone with the beautiful soup of the evening.

CLASSICS

Daniel E. Murphy

THIS TOO is a first-edition
Father did not buy in full
but paid half-off for he loved
other things more
like pagination

small printings
a slip-on/slip-off

clear book cover to wrap
the newest book a new purchase
an over-thumbed jacket
smelling of smoke
and spilled scotch

and muted debauchery

But I live local at the library
my adolescence grieved
in real time
in dusty silhouette fallen over
on *Reshelf* section

with truths ripped
from each dogeared page
I live for the smell of fealty
and determination
found elsewhere from home

using the master's tools to dismantle
his whole effing operation.

GOOD MORNING, HEARTACHE

Daniel E. Murphy

WASN'T IT ENOUGH to strip my house
under my very nose when I was young?
A thuggish doom invades our block of homes
slanted against each other in slum-like embrace,

our trees beggared of blooms and green—
their leaves a brash litter beneath.
                                        A loud mocking
from that tumbledown house sneaks onto the street
from hazy garage radios, engines revved

to hysteric heights that keep us inside
with women crying, a television fizzing.
Father is not here, he is out at all times
who comes home no more to our arms.

Father who fought another man's war and won,
but lost his way on his return—was it 10 years?
Or 10 lifetimes? My boyhood was wretched
like an old dock showing its ribs, underfed

with yearning and want and strife, my teeth
still sharpened with words, my nails cut
to flesh with the kitchen's dullest knife,
the hours pared into/from silent shadow.

HOMECOMING: *LUNA LUNERA*

Daniel E. Murphy

SEE AND SAY to my sweet heart
for God who loves me say to him
that I do not live of so much
suffering say to him he must
return to me his homecoming
postponed again how long I wait
under moonlight that I die
that he has compassion tell him
have mercy on my heart that
the scatterbrained moon shines
unequally on all

REVELATION

Daniel E. Murphy

IF THEY TELL YOU that he is dead
and gone, burn his gear, dig
a grave fit for young man
dressed in black, with coins

spread out around his fixed head
like CDs shimmering silver
and blue in sunlight.
That make a halo.

The dirt wet with tears.

                    Then return
ash to dirt, spread soil on skin
and funeral clothes. Let him live
in memory alone. Let him be.

And let the room
as his songs play on eternal

shuffle. Let the soul stray
from underworld to underworld
as friends pause, and let the drink
bless the soil his soul inhabits
with grieving god-men

beyond speech and laws
and impotent eyes.
And return to the dull
pursuits called Life.

IN COLD SILVER, LORCA

Daniel E. Murphy

AND LORCA was their spoon
for tasting, for parting and dishing out
to men in ties at 3:00 p.m.
There were no others of his worth—
all living poets too weak—the brave gone
into the great war, the maelstrom of *la frente*,
its grey oceans and dust-rattling ambulances.
The world of verse desiccated and grown
strange and diffident in coffin clothes.
Today the air was warm, the air was dry
and cool in half-light and dim corners:
a pool plashed and sauntered;
a stabled horse neighed, lonely
or maybe dreaming. Maybe inventing
a language to share later
with her midnight gypsy rider.
Lorca was their spoon, they needed
no knife or fork, and ate sherbet
with small silver they wiped
and used to stir espresso
in the grey-brown colonnade,
its late afternoon off-shadow.
They assembled
with Federico's mid-day grace
a meal and metronomic trance
set to 2/4 time, they all learned
to type and sip, to watch and dance,
and Lorca was the maestro, he
was the clock who set the time,

he led the dance always
and he was their spoon.

GITANO AMERICANO

Daniel E. Murphy

SLEEPWALK SERENADE—*romance*
en español—the torn love held
for her for him in both bright hands
like college-ruled homework sheets
we passed back and forth the 3 of us
high school friends the term
of love held 40 years ago 1979
Spanish Bombs came out 40 years
after the Spanish Civil War ended

it's 40 years now I loved green
que te quiero verde green branch
green root *verde viento* the 300 some
roses our dying anonymous soldier
dripped his necklace dripping red roses
blotched like plums he could not hold it
in hold it back was it life or art or death
he held on to leaving the botched body he held
his breath a gasp of foul air and steam
a small ghost maybe his self

No it was 300 black roses 3000
violet roses diamond tears a violent death
we at 18 registered for the draft 1979
1980 5 years after Vietnam the Spanish
alphabet has 30 letters or 29 depending
on your god or postal code or king's surname
the patriarch *santificado sea su nombre*

que se vaya al diablo el monstruo

We had one word we'd say to stop one word
you'd need to come one phrase it wasn't Spanish
it wasn't good English either not found in
Romancero Gitano not even *Poeta en Nueva York*
the soft newsprint pages our school copy
in your strong small hands that held affection
held me close held me

with nails bitten *to the quick and the dead* you said
held steady you turned licking each fingertip
turned your face, *a damaged copy* ON LOAN
you liked to say who liked *Canciones—*
small and terse like your thin body—the
the short musical shit the brittle pop melodies,
more than punk chords I could play or learned
as Time unfolded face cards falling in
fading with concert t-shirts worn out

a silk screen jumble in black and red on black
Get Yer Wings The Clash Take the Fifth
late nights learning diminished chords
scribbling out homework scraps of lyric
It's all genius like Beefheart the first shock
of Doc at the Radar Station the first hit
of infatuation those afternoons that mix
in the microwave
two tablespoons of Nescafé
two of sugar then half water and half milk
And who sleeps at night anyway

There was that shy one we shared
a gym locker for a semester he slept
a while a minute a century and counting now
we sat on the quad at lunch
on a side wall watched a band
of ants make a feast of a struggling bumble bee
someone had pulled its wings *for Science*

he sobbed almost silent we called him
Federico or manager accountant
our Boy Friday
later dressed in black suits
the ragged cuffs pulled out
he stood out

he sat in front in the señora's class fussing
anything to withdraw anything to please
everything turned in written in blue
to make the señora smile:

si fuera un rey
yo te envolvería en sábana blanca

Our Federico stood behind as we showed la maestra
London Calling played her Spanish Bombs
The señora: *¡Ay! ¡Qué horror! No es castellano.*

Then
Llevadme con vosotros—he cried
following us out of class grabbing me
her grabbing me
Lend me your ears you victims
of the conjugation of conditional verbs
Listen, I have seen the world beyond this school
he liked Berryman's voices Lowell's poem
about Miltown he found at Beyond Baroque
a long bus trip worth every sweaty second Daniel
The Book of Kabir *we're gonna need something*
some antidote something stronger to escape
este manicomio este Bellevue

Have you heard of Librium I found some
in my mother's purse she had it in a case of mints
Some afternoons we could sleep listening
to Bowie Low Side 2: We are all of us beautiful
in the dark, no? We can hold the pain at bay.

We can hold each other.

The world is the black horse
I am its dead rider.
Lorca wrote
Caballito negro, ¿Dónde llevas tu jinete muerto?

He signed his notes, *tu jinete vivo*
that last semester
he kept saying *I'm conjugating the past perfect*
the inflicted tense

then the preterite forever

and Federico dressed in blue
laid on his back
true to *imagination true to experience*
we tried to remember his first smile
was it real the words he wrote:

> we set our watch
> by poets' breath,
> morning's aspirations:
>
> our streets lined
> with mannequin bystanders
> like Plath's late-
>
> arriving doctors,
> a gun or blood
> gauge in each hand.
>
> Let's tell the truth—
> we like the danger,
> we like to watch
>
> but not feel gore
> splatter our breast

I slipped the handwritten poem I'd copied into his coat pocket
behind the rose clipped there fading too now
Who knows what grave melodies the earth will
sing after us after our bones what songs the first
Federico would have made with his life
would have made for our boy had he lived
beyond the war the halls painted baby blue
of C Building and high school's cyclical torture
este Bellevue nuestro Camarillo
and you and I the passionate dead lost
in books and newsprint facsimiles died
senior year he missed the Clash at the Palladium
missed prom missed the life he had rejected
he would have torn up anyway like that rose
still bleeding on the soldier's breast

But are we better now than we were then?
Kids on playgrounds in Ramones shirts
little girls and boys *The Future is Female*
Target's LGBTQ display in June

We say it could all be different it will
What words a poet could write to erase
the small misdiagnosis his quick step
out into air's vacuum its omission
a conversation no one can take back
not him not us she and I both holding
each other each held the note until
the melody broke in sharp hissing of waves
and her handwriting *el barco sobre la mar*
(from Lorca of course) its blue dampening
in the ocean's green-brown lap and curl.

FICCIÓN

GAME

Majo Delgadillo

IT'S NOT SCARY if it's a game. It's not scary if you remember we're playing. Count to ten between each breath, *one Mississippi, two Mississippis, three Mississippis...* Whisper. Don't make a sound. It's not a threat, I just don't want to hear that voice right now. I'm not interested in the pleading. It's not scary if you remember we're about to eat. We're sitting at the table facing the wonders of pleasure, remember? We're smelling pepper and cinnamon. Sage. Game. It's not scary if we hold hands and I tell you a story: *Once upon a time lived a poor woodcutter with his wife and his two children. The boy's name was Hansel and the girl's name was Gretel. He had but little to eat, and once, when a great famine came to the land, he could no longer provide even their daily bread.* It's not scary if you remember what happens next: the woodcutter will take the siblings to the forest to try to get rid of them. The boy leaves traces behind, remember? First round, they come back. Like zombies. Like the undead. A hungry plague, a crying curse, the children. Second round, they get lost and find the house of a witch. They don't know she's a witch, remember? They just know the house is made of sweets and sugar. A dream. The story won't say it, but they'll wonder if they're dead. If this is paradise. The siblings, who have only known their own hunger, a pull in their guts, a scream stuck in their throats, the sickly quality of honey over their tongues; they will find a new kind of pleasure when they learn the act of sinking teeth. They bite, remember? It's not scary if you remember. It's not scary if you know the story. They open their mouths to eat whole universes. They chew on the foundations of the house. They swallow the frosting and the colors. They realize they're not dead. They realize they have never been this alive. And just when they're finally satisfied, like a selfish king and queen, the witch finds them. In the story, the witch will find them and bring them home. New toys or foraged mushrooms, the children. And the witch will sing to them: songs, lullabies. She will tell them stories before bed. She won't be angry. She will desire to keep them. This is the part the story always gets wrong. She's maternal, the witch. More attentive and certain of what they need. Feeding them. Holding their hands, and wiping pearls of sweat from their foreheads when they get sick. That's the part the story gets wrong. She loved them, remember? It's not scary if you remember the days they would spend together, singing and dancing. In a haze. In love. The story gets this part wrong. In it, the witch transforms the little girl. No longer a sister but a torturer, remember? An executioner, fattening up the brother like a suckling pig and dreaming of dying. *Oh, how the poor little sister sobbed "Dear God, please help us," she cried. "If only the wild animals had devoured us in the woods, then we would have died together"*. It's not scary if you remember that the story is wrong. It's not scary if you remember that we had rules and regulations and prizes and love. It's not scary if you remember the frenzy of dancing, the sensation of an expanded belly after eating cream and berries. The fingers over your ribcage and inside your mouth. The other kinds of hunger: salivating at the sight of lips or of legs. This is what the story gets wrong: we had rules. A pact set up one morning, the gold of sunlight rippling through handmade curtains. The witch stares at her children, grown and ripe, who request a game. And she accepts. It's not scary if you remember we're playing a game and games have rules. It's not scary if you think about the rules: a bite for a bite. A hunger for a hunger. A hunger, in fact, in exchange for two satiated little kids. The witch, is true, has been hungry. The witch has always been too hungry for this world. Too hungry with desire, a fever for feasts and festivals. The witch feeds the children: sweets and roasted meat and marshmallows. It was morning when we set up the rules, the sun coming in through the windows, remember? And I told you the truth: a bite for a bite. This is a part of the story that's unfair. It's true that the witch wants to sink her own teeth into flesh and bone. Breaking. Pulling. Swallowing. It's true that the witch dreams of the nerves trapped between the gaps in her mouth. White strings of gummy flesh giving in. But it's unfair to say that the witch turns the girl into a torturer. She just allows for passion to have room to roam. It's not scary if I bring you close to my chest, *shhhshhh.* It's not scary if I call you my love. My love, you know what's coming. The decisive moment. A breakthrough: becoming a victim or a murderer. Becoming the sizzling of fat above an open flame. It's not scary if we're playing a game: hide and seek, cat and mouse. I'll close my eyes and count to ten between each breath. It's not scary if I remind you of your role: your brother will attempt to run. His legs, round and fleshy, will make a supple sound where the thighs meet and you'll signal to your hands and your legs and your tongue. To go. To not salivate. But you won't be able to avoid it. It's not scary if you're under a spell. It's not scary if it's beautiful. A banquet in candlelight. A kiss on the lips. It's not scary if you're in love, my love. It's not scary if you cook it right, the flesh coming off the bone, softly, juicy. The smell of burnt hair covered by butter and honey. It's not scary if you sip on wine and mead. It's not scary if you remember your wishes: we are the wild animals. We can die together. And you're hungry, remember? You were so hungry you could eat a house. It was a time of great famine, and you could've eaten an entire village. You could've turned into teeth, a cannibal. I understand. I do. You want to know what it feels like, being an only child. Becoming my wild thing. Hungry and sticky with sugared fingers. You want to know what it's like to be a creature of pure desire. So eat. Open your mouth. It's the rules of this game. A hunger for a hunger.

BORRACHOS HOLDING HAND

Ryan Kulcak

TO WALK IN HOUSTON was to die. To take the METRO was to die twice over; once from the stab wound and again from the inevitable infection. Having survived so far, though, I made my way on a well trod path in the grass through a transient state of matter the local weatherman called 100% humidity. The warm gulf air came from just far enough away that it didn't smell of salt, but it intensified everything else's scent. On tonight's nose menu was exhaust and a Chinese taco truck I'd never quite worked up the courage to try.

Buffalo Bayou vaguely resembled something of a natural waterway here just outside the inner loop. The marshland alongside it sank with each of my steps. It was a workout just lifting my feet out of the vacuums my weight created in the ground. Shhhhhloop, ffrrrrrroop. My faux gator skin boots would've been sucked into the ground long ago if I hadn't kept my toes pointing upwards. They were my only pair of shoes left except for my non-slip crocs I'd had to buy for work. They'd saved my ass several times after only three weeks at Whataburger.

Fences and concrete walls surrounded the bayou in this area, sometimes brick walls if there was a particularly rich neighborhood on the other side of it. The city made sure to save the ugliest banks for those who dared to have easily climbable metal fences. I spotted then grappled the black rods in front of the place I usually went through. The small, familiar yard was filled with the same rusted junk, tools, and fridges. Why were there always fridges?

Before I even saw it, a German Shepherd barked like it personally wanted to sever my jugular. Leaping from behind one of the rusted tool boxes, it gave me a look like it could already taste my ass. Incoherently cursing under my breath, I made a break for the side gate. No time to bother opening it this time. I made a jump for it and clumsily landed on top and knocked the gate off its upper hinge. The dog nabbed the seam of a pant leg and kept it as I yanked my leg over the fence.

Once in the front yard I heard an old woman yelling something in Spanish from inside the house. A teenager came outside shaking something in the air and yelled at me across the street, "Nunca vuélvete aquí más, chingo chino cochino! Nunca!"

Before making it around an intersection I yelled back with megaphone hands, "Soy más mexicano que las empanadas de tu madre! Ya sé porque soy tu papi!"

Turning around one last time, I saw him fly the bird high and proud while gripping his balls just a little too hard in my direction. Seems I'd have to find a different route for tomorrow's meeting. Too many damn dogs in these areas. Chingas perras. Once out of the neighborhood, it was only a few more blocks to the club. Was a relief to be walking under street lights again. Didn't stop me from chronically checking over my shoulder, though.

The night sky was always the same dull gray in the city. It'd been many years since I'd last seen even a decent amount of stars in the sky. That'd been while visiting family outside of Đà Nẵng to attend the funeral of my last living ancestor in Vietnam. After my great-grandmother died, my only direct ancestors left besides mama were my grandparents in Guadalajara. Mama considered it a cultural necessity to always have at least two bottles of Valentina in the house at all times. To do otherwise would be an insult a la patria. Not quite as bad as flying the gold star instead of the three red stripes. I'd never dared to utter the name Hồ Chí Minh in the presence of my father. All I knew that respect was that, in some manner or another, he'd been responsible for the deaths of my father's parents. Dad'd been long dead before I'd given his side of my family story the respect it deserved.

It was by the highway lights that I saw yet another symbol that'd come to mean much to me the past year. In the second story window of a stripmall presbyterian church was a red circle perfectly encompassing a triangle of the same color. Plain, nondescript, subtle. Anonymous, one might say. Though I could never quite tune out the deafening roar of the cars speeding by, just the sight of this place produced a sort of serenity in me; a calm that I couldn't explain. The strip had become more of a home to me than any other place I'd been since me and mama'd had to leave the house back in '09.

I'd understood very little of what was going on at the time, especially since most of Hidalgo st. went through the same ordeal. We were not the exception. Eating PB&J home alone while my parents took on extra shifts was normal. Had over the neighbors to pass the time almost everyday. Seeing the shame on my father's face, though; the helplessness of my mother coming home from her second job with almost nothing to show for it; the reeking black spots and missing sections of drywall after Ike came through; the piles of foreclosure notices we pretended didn't exist. That's what the word "recession" came to mean to me.

I'd mostly kept to just inside the loop and I-10 area since being in recovery. Not only was this just a few blocks from old Hidalgo st, it was also within walking distance (if one were to, say, trespass through some "private property" and ignore the absurd jaywalking laws of Houston) of El Camino Club of Alcoholics Anonymous. I'd been introduced to the place through Houston Behavioral's addiction treatment facility. Within AA everyone knew what you meant when you said "treatment facility." Otherwise, though, I always had to say "rehab" or I'd get a confused tilt of the head. After all we'd put our pride and self-esteem through, calling it rehab was just a bit too much for our eager egos. They lay just under the surface, ready to take back the reins and end us back up in one institution or another.

As I neared the stairs, two men on the balcony nodded towards me as a hello. I'd not yet noticed the cigarette ashes they'd tapped onto me from above. After rising to the second story and wiping my shoulders clean of debris, I lifted my open hand in the universal "duh fuk" sign. As practiced many times over, this smoothly transitioned into a clasp of our hands and I hugged Paul over a good laugh.

I tried not to make too much eye contact with the other one, Carlo. He'd always managed to wriggle his way into every conversation I had in the same room as him. I knew he wasn't violent, but anytime he broke out into his schizophrenic word salad I never quite knew what to say or do except nod and act as if he hadn't just asked me, "How's the institution of property going to transmit legally with your wife? She's doing electrolytes and serenity in the second coming, right? I knows the second coming, man. We done the first, now we waitin for the third."

"My lady's doing fine, Carlo. Thanks for asking." I said.

I'd been single since I'd met him. Maybe he meant mama? She'd come to an open meeting with me once, God save her. He might've seen her there, assumed I had myself a supportive cougar. Last thing I need my sobriety to depend on.

"There's coffee in the lobby if you want some." Paul offered.

"When is there ever not coffee?" I said, genuinely trying to remember if I'd ever been to a meeting without an old, stained coffee pot. No such memory came to mind. I knew many who didn't drink coffee unless they went to AA. Almost a bitter Eucharist wine at this point.

I walked inside, saying hello to an old, black puertorriqueño whose English was but a garbled, welcoming bellow. I understood his Spanish perfectly, yet he never spoke his native tongue with my chino lookin ass. I always nodded and smiled over a handshake, often considering responding with something along the lines of, "qué tal, negrito viejo?" Today just wasn't the day.

Upon entering the bathroom I saw a sign listing what not to flush down the toilet written in English, Spanish (the essentials), Vietnamese, Korean, Hindi, some other Asian script I didn't recognize, and what was presumably Igbo or Yoruba. The Presbytarians were very protective of their toilet, yet only let us host thirteen meetings a week;

ten in English and three in Spanish (alternately titled "El Grupo de La Manera"). I guess the Asians and Nigerians were expected to hold their own meetings in the bathroom. Maybe the masjid next door held one for Hausa speakers.

I noticed something black and crumpled underneath the sink: a half full bottle of Black Box. Looked like someone needed some lubricant before stepping back into the rooms. If I were to assume the best (which you should never do with alcoholics), I'd say they'd been trying to get through the delirium tremens without dying from a seizure. I threw it away, paused, thought, then took it back out to pour what was left down the sink. I couldn't stand wine, let alone warm shitty white wine out of a box found in the bathroom. To an alcoholic having a rough day in early recovery, though, that may end up being the beginning of their last and worst binge.

I'd never been to one of those circle-of-fold-up-chairs-in-the-gymnasium-type meetings like in the movies before. Neither was there usually crying. Usually, that is. Sometimes people had a fucked up day or week or year and needed to have a good fucking cry so they could get back to feeling able to exist. The fold up chairs were there, though. Two in the front: one for the chair of the meeting, the other for the lead. If you were lucky the lead was down to earth and knew how to translate his week's experience into a good, relevant topic. If you were unlucky, however, you'd either get someone who went on a twenty minute drunkalog or thought they were being original by asking themself if they'd *truly* accepted that they were powerless over alcohol and couldn't manage their life. Those types always ended with, "Well, hopefully you got a good topic out of my rambling."

No. No I did not, asshole

This was not one of those meetings. A man wearing a vaquero tejano hat and plaid sat down in the lead seat. He jumped out when Beto told him to get his Mexican ass out of his chair. Beto was a proudly American man of Mexican descent who called every Hispanic a shade darker than him un mojado. Except for me, that was, since I was his chinito cabrón.

Did I ever correct him? No.

Should I have? Also probably no.

Me and Beto didn't know each other well in the sense that most friends do. AA buddies are a different kind. We knew and shared different things about ourselves than we would in any other context. We talked about the realities of drinking and the shit it'd brought upon our lives. Beto didn't even know I hadn't had a drink since I was nineteen. I'd smoked a shit ton of crack in the years since, though. Have to be careful about talking about drugs, lest some oldtimer cross talks your share. Best to avoid it if not familiar with the meeting.

"Hey, asshole! No smoking inside! Get your ass to the balcony. Minister is going to lay a brick if he smells that shit in here." said Beto to a woman in the back in the most respectful tone he could muster. She proceeded to threaten Beto while walking backwards to the door, puffing as much smoke into the room as possible before closing the door. Maybe the wine had been hers.

"And with that, let's get this shit started."

I almost never shared unless called on. Always felt like there was someone else who needed to more or had something better to say. Least I could do is listen, though. These people, for some reason or another, had decided to place their trust in the room to be audience to their deepest worries and concerns, their guilt and shame, the daily joys of waking up sober and experiencing life as a decent human being, the sometimes deep abyss that was losing someone in the first year of recovery. None of it should be taken for granted. When I came in on shitty days, stuck in my head and feeling sorry for myself, the only thing that helped me out was to focus on the words of others and just being present for them.

Today that meant listening to Michelle speak about whether or not she could stay with her husband. He was an alcoholic too and still brought booze into the house. When there wasn't any around, she could still smell it on his breath. Sometimes Michelle had sex with him just to taste and smell it on his breath. It was too much of a temptation.

But how could she leave him? They had layers of debt together and two young children to think of. She'd lose all of her family and possessions if she didn't put her sobriety first, though, Michelle reminded herself. She didn't know what to do, but somehow or another, if she surrendered herself her higher power would take care of the rest, she said.

Thanks, Michelle.

Everyone slowly nodded, making themselves feel good by agreeing with her final words of wisdom. Here's our experience and support, yes, but we need to feel involved in your survival. Let's focus on you and your solution so that I may find mine.

Beto called on a skinny, timid man in the back who responded with an almost inaudible, "I'm just listening tonight." I kept an eye on him. A fresh one.

Thanks.

The next fifteen minutes were spent listening to the usuals. This group of mostly white middle aged to elderly men sat either in the front or side of the room everyday. They all had at least five years of sobriety, sometimes a decade or two.

Charles, the lone black man amongst the old timer crowd at this meeting, held a steep lead of forty-three years. Him getting his forty-third chip last month had been something of a holiday for the El Camino group. Charles was a sign of hope that all this shit was worth it. That we might truly be capable of becoming the people we wanted to be. Old timer shares were always the same shit, though. I was sick, I came here, now I'm better, and I'm only better today because I kept up the work everyday of my life since then. Good for the newcomers, that's for sure (remembering, I turn to look at the man in the back. Good, still there), but I'd heard the same shit a million times.

Thanks, Charles.

A younger man near the front named Vicente volunteered and shared that his sponsor had assigned his fourth step two weeks ago and hadn't been able to get himself to touch it once. He knew every single resentment he needed to write down, but his father had to be the first. Had to be. Vicente had no idea how he could possibly put into words the years and years of shit into just a couple paragraphs. It'd be a novel. Where would he even start? The thought of it all made him feel sick inside. He knew he was just stalling, though. His sponsor had told him as much. He made a pact with himself to sit down with a notebook and write until he couldn't write anymore. Only way he could make it happen. It had to happen.

Thanks, Vicente.

A few more shares later and the meeting was over. When the call went out for twenty-four hour chips our newbie went up to grab one. Beto shook his hand after handing it to him, asked his name, then called out to the room, "Miles, everyone! Miles!"

Beto went through the rounds. A couple grabbed a one month chip, another grabbed a three month. The moment I'd been pretending not to wait for the whole night came around when I heard the call for eight months. A round of applause went up around the room as I rose to my feet. The clapping always felt different when it was for you. Beto surprised me with a hug, a rarity for him. Everyone I passed by nodded their heads or shook my hand or fist bumped me. It was over in thirty seconds, but sometimes that half minute made the past thirty days so much more worthwhile.

As we finished with an Our Father, I looked around the circle of borrachos holding hands to find Miles. He was nowhere to be found. I snatched a copy of the mens' phone number list and ran out the room. I leaned over the balcony and saw Miles' small figure hopping onto a bike.

"Miles, wait! Don't forget your number list." I called across the parking lot. He looked back with a look of confusion and a tinge of bitterness. These were not unique emotional responses to the jovial vibes of one's first AA meeting. Making my way down the stairs and across the lot I held out the piece of paper to the young man, begging him with my eyes to take it.

“You’ll need it, man. Don’t be afraid to call somebody if you need to, or even if you don’t need to. I’m on the list, #27. I hope to see you again.”

His face slackened a little, his initial suspicion breaking away to allow a small but genuine smile.

“For real, call me. You’ll need it. Helps me more than it helps you.” I almost cringed at repeating the same slogans I’d so despised just last year.

“I will.” Miles said back, then he rode away into the night.

In all likelihood, he wouldn’t. In fact, he might have been on his way to get wasted there and then. Maybe he already was. No real way of knowing. I just knew that I felt better for having made the offer known to him. In reality I had no real obligation to anyone in AA, but I most certainly did owe them. Even the ones who didn’t know it yet.

It was late, foggy, and this wasn’t quite the place to be walking around in the middle of the night. I didn’t particularly want to, but I caught a ride home with Carlo. He may baffle me in conversation, but the guy was more generous than most people around him ever deserved. As soon as I asked he broke out in a big smile. No worries about awkward conversations in the car either. He was about 92.59% sure the CIA had tapped his car after he’d sent a threatening letter to a former Kuwaiti ambassador to the United States.

Our little sober living home looked quite out of place amongst the rows of three story townhouses that lined the rest of the street. Most of the gentrification around here had happened before I moved in, but even in the last eight months I’d seen old mom and pops leave the block with a check in hand. Our new “neighbors” were not fans of our existence despite them being the intruders. We got HOA notices in the mail at least once a week for supposed violations.

Upon arriving home I silently thanked Carlo with a wave as I closed the door. A cop stared me down from the cul-de-sac, waiting for an excuse. I did not give him one. He’d approached me coming home at night several times, hoping to find some dope on me. He'd given up after I'd been in for a month.

Walking up the porch steps, I knew Michael would be waiting there on the other side of the door. Thankfully, he'd decided not to jump out and scare me as he often did when I arrived home late.

Tapping his watch, he said, "Two minutes late. Tsk, tsk, tsk, buddy. Woulda had a strike if I didn't trust your ass."

"Que amable." I retorted back. I was glad to be home until I saw his face. It was completely off: sunken, apathetic, done with the day for the next couple weeks. Something was very wrong.

"Que pasó? Porque la mirada?" I asked, dreading the answer.

"Tanner está muerto. Overdosed in a parking lot down the road. Shot up una cosa en la que fue fent. Su familia sacó sus cosas hoy temprano."

All I could see or feel or think of was the bedside picture of Tanner's eight year old daughter I'd seen everyday for the last eight months. It wouldn't be there ever again. I hoped she'd done well in her soccer tournament yesterday. Tanner said she'd been so excited.

THE PAPYROMANCER'S APPRENTICE

Blake Sanz

AFTER THE INCIDENT, she made paper from scratch in the garage of a Florida bungalow. She snipped wildrye she'd gathered from the swamp and boiled it like tea, then beat it to a pulp on a makeshift workstation fashioned from cinder blocks. Into a plastic container that had once held the necessities of a first-aid kit, she poured the pulp and added water, then ran the mixture through a beater. She'd made her own deckles—one for envelopes and one for eight by eight squares—with scrap wood left in a pile behind a home goods store, approximating forms she found on YouTube, and when the pulp felt evenly mixed, she dipped the deckles one by one into the green substance, shaking out the excess by moving it forward and back, left and right, up and down, over and over until an even, green mass appeared in the molds and her arms were as tired as they had been that night.

After an hour's rest she placed a wet sheet on a felt square with a cinder block atop it and repeated the process ten times, one for each sheet, making a tall stack of weight and potential. The next morning, she ran a clothesline from a fence post to a crepe myrtle and hung the speckled-green sheets with clothespins to fully dry in the sun. Beneath a live oak heavy with moss, a free-standing clawfoot was rusting in the yard. Pitying the tub its forced embrace of her immigrant body, she lay in it with a magazine about housekeeping and practiced her English by reading about a method by which one might eliminate char on frying pans by sprinkling it with baking soda and rubbing the burn with tin foil. In America, this was the time when she was happiest.

The next day when the sheets were dry, she plucked them from the line and stacked them neatly. Adapting as best she could, thinking of the conventions of papyromancy her grandmother had once outlined, she used a felt-tip pen to draw a pattern onto the paper in a carefully articulated progression of leaf shapes and tessellated birds, sunspots and starbursts. These, she vaguely remembered, corresponded to prayers of asking. She drew each form slowly, the fresh sheet allowing the ink to bleed into blots here and there. She creased the paper at right angles and diagonals, cutting it in places so she could undertake the folds that would transform the sheet into a dimensional object of art and divination—in this case, a paper ashtray replete with divots at each corner for the civilized resting of fags. It looked like something her father might have used in those times when, finished for the day with his dentistry practice in Poza Rica, he would smoke a cigar on the front stoop and tell stories about Castro and the revolution. The patterns of her inking revealed themselves in the surfaces of the paper that faced outward. When finished she placed the tiny ashtray on the wrought iron of a patio table. Admired it briefly. Then, fold by fold, she undid her work until the paper was flat again. Later, she thought, after she had found a way back to Veracruz, after she had finally arrived in the house from which she'd fled, she would check the mailbox to find this relic of her time here in the north. Only then would she begin the process of divination that would lead to her final unmasking—the rediscovery of her true self that had been lost in coming here—according to the amate rituals of that region, rituals she had figured so recently to discard for the sake of the convenience of a Target. The allure of name brands. Or maybe, despite the rape, she would stay here after all. Maybe God was waiting in the folds of a piece of paper she could buy from a strip mall.

She scored a second sheet that had emerged from the deckle meant for making envelopes, folded its triangled edges so that it took its intended form. On the outside, she wrote her name and childhood address: *A____, 29612 San Pablito; Veracruz, Mex. 29876.* Her family had been killed there amid a wave of cartel violence. She had fled, and now that house was empty, and there would be no reason to ransack it again, but could the rooms themselves be a comfort? A new starting point? Maybe the ashtray could tell her. She did not yet place the inked paper in the newly-made envelope, instead picked it up and examined it. Noted where the creases intersected with leaf shapes and birdwings. Her grandmother would know what all this meant. Perhaps her grandmother would teach her such things, but this could only happen in person. In San Pablito. Or else, maybe a Magic Eight-Ball was the same thing, and this hardest of all returns, backwards to the place of her origins, would be for nothing. Maybe the future was blank. Or maybe, in some future moment post re-arrival, after she'd found her grandmother and after some apprenticing, her little ashtray would be ready by then to tell the future. *Lilliya,* it might say then, addressing the her that knew how to hold such a wonder: *here is what will be.*

ALGUNA VEZ EN UN CUARTO AZUL

Anjanette Delgado

Traducido del inglés por Antonio Díaz Oliva (ADO)

> *Si el mundo juzga, con ojos cerrados/ y todo lo que hago es un pecado/ Pero si tú lo tienes todo controlado/ ¿Por qué me temes? ¿A qué le temes?*
>
> —Ile, de su canción, "Temes", 2019

TIEMPO DESPUÉS, las personas culparían al azul. Sí, sí, al color azul. Que si bien estaban al tanto de que un simple color no podía ser el responsable de algo así, igual insistían en describir aquella noche y cómo era que era el tal azul, y que no, que no se referían al cielo, sino a la noche misma, esa que había chorreado tinta por los cuatro costados de aquel pueblo, por sobre las chozas y los graneros y las parcelas de tierra que les pertenecían, en aquella noche que comenzó con la mujer en cuestión sentada en el piso de su dormitorio, escupiendo sangre como un tractor averiado habría escupido barro.

La habitación quedaba en la parte trasera de la casa en la que la mujer y su esposo vivían con la madre del esposo y con el marido de la madre del esposo, y ahí había estado ella sentada, estrujándose las manos e intentando tragarse los alaridos que había convertido en murmullos, pero que insistían en querer salir, ahogándola, subiendo por su garganta como la bilis una, y otra, y otra vez.

La gente le contaba, incluso a perfectos desconocidos y, la verdad, a cualquiera que quisiera escuchar, que la enfermera que había testificado por televisión no tenía nada que ver. Que si se iba a ser justo, entonces había que admitir que sí era posible, porque todo es posible, que el culpable de todo lo ocurrido fuera el azul. Que durante aquella noche violenta —mientras la mujer en el piso se preguntaba si era posible quedar daltónico a causa de eventos desafortunados, si el caso era que esos eventos desafortunados ocurrían con frecuencia—

hubiese sido el azul y no la enfermera ni sus palabras, sino aquel azul intenso como las profundidades del océano Pacífico que ellos nunca verían con sus propios ojos (pero que podían imaginar) el que se había metido en aquella habitación trasera como si quisiera ser la respuesta a las preguntas que la mujer se hacía en su mente.

Que el azul ese se le había metido por dentro haciéndose pasar por oxígeno, causando que el pecho de ella se hinchara con un respirar ruidoso que nadie oyó, haciéndole la cabeza niebla, volviéndola estúpida, incapaz de discernir entre lo que era qué y lo que no.

Aquella había sido una de esas noches en las que cosas malas pueden pasar, y pasan, entre una mujer y su marido. Solo que a la mujer y a su esposo esas cosas malas habían comenzado a sucederles cada vez más a menudo, y tal vez eso se combinó con el azul para que después de que terminó la primera cosa mala, y terminó también una segunda cosa mala que se suscitó sin que la mujer entendiera cómo, todo se hiciera silencio, hasta la respiración, y fue como si el esposo de la mujer ya no estuviera ahí, aunque ahí estaba, espatarrado sobre la cama, dormido profundo, más allá del sueño y tan quieto que ni sus ronquidos podían escucharse.

Fue entonces cuando ella se recogió a sí misma del piso y se paró junto a la única ventana de la habitación, el interior de su magullado labio inferior latiendo como un corazón.

Y debe haber sido justo ahí que el azul la llamó a través de la ventana y la convenció de ir a la cocina, de servirse un vaso de agua de la llave, de escuchar con atención antes de abrir la puerta trasera con más sigilo que nunca, para encontrarse con él, con el azul, allá afuera, ella con sus chancletas plásticas color marrón, las manos en los bolsillos de su falda de algodón verde.

Y para ser justos, porque la gente de aquel pueblo siempre trataba de ser justa, ellos concedían que existía la posibilidad de que la mujer hubiese estado siguiendo al azul cuando cruzó el sendero cubierto de gravilla que llevaba hasta el frente de la casa, que era donde quedaban todas las demás habitaciones, un pie delante del otro, ella bien casual, como quien no quiere la cosa, pero con cuidado, para no despertar ni a su suegra ni al marido de su suegra si sus pies golpeaban sin querer alguna de las muchas herramientas oxidadas, de las llantas y tuercas tiradas por doquier, cualquier movimiento, capaz de crear un estrépito metálico si es que tenía la mala suerte de tropezar con ellas mientras cruzaba aquel patio lleno de macetas de arcilla pobladas solo de yerbamala.

Sin embargo, y en esto la gente sí que no transaba: si todo lo anterior era posible, entonces había que admitir que asimismo era posible, es más, que era hasta probable, que sí hubiese sido idea de la mujer hacer lo que hizo con "intención premeditada", así como también con algo llamado en inglés "men's rea", lo cual la gente escuchó en la televisión sin entender, porque si bien sabían que "men" significa hombres, y que la apóstrofe y la "s" significaban posesión, igual no se explicaban qué carajos era un "rea", ni quiénes eran aquellos hombres a quienes supuestamente les pertenecía.

Pero, ¿cuál era la verdad? La mujer recordaba que había sido su idea, y no la del azul, aquello de caminar como por casualidad, sin destino ni dirección, hasta pasar el punto donde ya no habría sido factible decir que no se había dado cuenta, que había estado caminando distraída, pensando en esto y en aquello sin percatarse de lo lejos de la casa que sus pasos la habían llevado, ni de lo oscura de la noche. Que había sido su idea caminar sin pensar mucho si continuar por ahí o doblar por allá cosa de que, si era atrapada, fuera la pura verdad que había sido culpa de su mente despistada, y nada más, lo que la llevó al límite de la propiedad como si intentara escapar.

Así caminó durante un rato largo, la mujer, escuchando a lo lejos el sonido que hacían las ramas de los árboles del campo intentando abrazar al viento, y el que hacían los grillos y los pájaros y las otras cosas que Dios creó solo para verlas arrastrarse toda una vida por el suelo, la suciedad y la muerte de esta tierra. Había caminado y escuchado durante un rato largo, asombrada de poder oírlo todo, hasta el más leve crujido bajo sus pies.

Caminando pasó también por delante de casas y graneros y a través del desorden de patios ajenos llenos de cosas viejas, desechas hacía tiempo ya. Cruzó granjas cercadas y bajó por senderos enmarcados por matojos hasta que hubo sudor entre sus pechos, pero los dedos de sus pies eran diez frágiles estalactitas.

Caminaba sin pensar en nada en especial. Quizás solo en Lilly, la perra sata de su infancia, aquella que, ciega de nacimiento, igual se las arregló para amarla más y mejor de lo que ser humano vidente alguno la había amado jamás, y así pensando, para cuando escuchó la música y vio las luces naranjas a lo lejos, ya no podía sentir sus pies, solo su cabeza palpitando donde él había agarrado la costumbre de golpearla de manera que su cabello escondiera un cuero cabelludo teñido de zarzamoras a fuerza de golpes.

Entonces caminó lentamente hacia el letrero que decía "El Bar de Eva", la música que salía del interior del lugar tan fuerte que la mujer la sintió en todas partes: detrás de la cuenca de sus ojos, en la concavidad de sus oídos e incluso en el punto preciso que servía de eje a sus muslos.

Quería sentarse. Necesitaba sentarse y aquel letrero de neón naranja era una muy buena señal si significaba que en estos lares una mujer podía ser dueña de cosas e incluso ponerles su nombre en un letrero a la vista de todos.

Y si bien algo de silencio le hubiera venido bien a su cabeza pulsante, decidió arreglárselas sin él porque, total, ¿cuándo había hecho el silencio algo por alguien? Ella venía de un lugar donde los bebés nacían de niñas a las cuales aún les faltaba mucho para convertirse en mujeres y nadie decía nada, ni hacía mucho ruido y nada cambiaba. Ella conocía mujeres que pasaban sus vidas yendo de aquí para allá sin levantar la vista excepto para silenciar a cualquiera que osara reír, o jugar, o llorar mientras un hombre dormía dentro de sus casas silenciosas. ¿Y qué hizo alguna vez por ellas toda aquella quietud? ¿Qué había hecho por pueblos enteros llenos de gente con secretos tan grandes y terribles que ni a Dios se los podían contar?

Cuando hubo respirado hasta componerse, la mujer, que llevaba muy poco tiempo siéndolo, fingió una sonrisa y entró en aquella ruidosa semioscuridad con firmeza, con seguridad, a pesar de lo estrujadas de su falda verde olivo línea A y de su blusa color marrón como sus chancletas. Se paró en la entrada y esperó a que la gente sentada en la barra la mirara todo lo que quisiera antes de regresar a sus tragos y a la pantalla de televisor que, en este lugar, era un rectángulo gigantesco de coloridas imágenes en movimiento, suspendida sobre el enorme círculo alargado de la barra que habían colocado en el mismo centro del local.

—¿Dónde quieres sentarte, mi vida? Cariño, ¿todo bien? ¡Cariño! ¿Mesa o barra? —la apuró una camarera de jeans ajustados y cabello oscuro, corto y puntiagudo, que, pese a la bandeja repleta de tragos que cargaba en uno de sus brazos, se había acercado bordeando la esquina del local como si estuviera montada en patines.

A manera de respuesta, la mujer apuntó hacia la barra, antes de atravesar la densa neblina azul del bar para sentarse en el taburete que había señalado.

De inmediato, el bartender puso una servilleta frente a ella sin detenerse a preguntarle qué deseaba, pasando raudo frente a la media docena de manos extendidas a lo largo de la barra, su cara escondida por la neblina azul, su velocidad a la par de la de la camarera.

La mujer sabía que lucía más o menos normal. (De algo servía que él siempre se hubiese preocupado tanto por golpearla estratégicamente). Pero no tenía dinero y se preguntó si eso sería algo que el camarero sí detectaría, y si, de hacerlo, le pediría que se fuera.

Buscando alternativas, vio un letrero en forma de flecha que decía "baño" y apuntaba hacia una esquina cuyo contorno era indistinguible en la oscuridad. El letrero parecía estar suspendido sobre la nada y no decía ni "hombres" ni "mujeres". Cualquiera podía usarlo. El lavamanos tendría agua, y adentro habría un basurero para eso que llevaba en su bolsillo izquierdo, aquello todavía cubierto por la bolsa plástica que ella había tomado de la cocina antes de salir. Tal vez podría quedarse en ese baño hasta que cerraran, para evitar tener que pedir algo de beber, pensó, y estaba a punto de bajar del taburete cuando un hombre a su lado gritó por sobre la algarabía, "Mikey, una cerveza para la dama", antes de volverse hacia ella y ofrecerle la mano.

—Mayra—respondió la mujer como si así se llamara, pero tardando tanto en responder que él había estado a punto de darle la espalda, asumiendo que no estaba interesada en conocer a nadie con quien divertirse.

—Pues encantado, Mayra. Ismael. ¿Eres de por acá? —dijo él acercando tanto su boca a la oreja de ella para ser escuchado por encima del ruido, que ella sintió sus palabras en todos los lugares del cuerpo en los que antes había sentido la música del bar y le parecieron una invasión.

Además, no había previsto preguntas de nadie, y no quería responder algo sin tener la oportunidad de pensar, de sopesarlo todo un minuto siquiera, así que solo sonrió y apretó los dedos de los pies para estabilizarse, ahora que habían entrado en calor y podía sentirlos de nuevo.

Él sonrió también, pero su expresión era de respuesta, como si la sonrisa de ella fuera un reto que él estaba aceptando. Le dijo que era asiduo a aquel bar, que iba todos los días después del trabajo, y que por eso sabía que ella nunca había estado allí antes, y que no era de los alrededores.

Ella quiso responder algo, pero hubo un alboroto repentino de la gente en el bar en respuesta a la anotación de uno de los equipos. El ruido hizo que su cuerpo entero se encogiera y que el Ismael aquel se diera vuelta gritando "Wepa!" y "Esa es la que hay, papá. ¡Chúpate esa!", sus ojos de pronto pegados a la pantalla, la mujer repentinamente de vuelta en su dormitorio en la parte trasera de la casa de su suegra y ahora toda la gente que veía el juego estaba ahí, en su casa, y de la habitación de su suegra salían los ruidos del bar, como si ella no se hubiera movido en toda la noche y estuviera todavía sentada en el piso de su habitación, observando personajes entrar y salir de escena, solo los ruidos cambiando alrededor de ella con cada subir y caer del telón, o con cada anotación de un jugador.

Y no es que ella fuera fanática del deporte, ni que estuviera familiarizada con los lugares a los cuales la gente acudía para divertirse, pero aquella era una noche azul y tal vez por eso ella entendió que lo que estaba viendo y entendiendo era que había mujeres, como las que estaban en aquel bar, que sí eran felices y no solo fingiendo serlo. Mujeres que se sentían cómodas gritándole a un televisor en una barra pública, tomando cervezas, y sonriéndole a hombres llamados Ismael. Mujeres que sí tenían opciones y podían ser amigas de los ruidos provenientes de noches tan azules como aquella que la había empujado a ella a escapar horas antes, golpeada y sudorosa y ocultándose de una madre que amaba tanto a su hijo que insistía en defenderlo por encima de todo.

Ahora Ismael hablaba con alguien que estaba en su costado opuesto y, era obvio, no le había mentido cuando le dijo que era cliente habitual allí, que pertenecía al lugar y todos lo conocían. Ella se preguntó cómo se sentiría aquello de tener amigos, de pertenecer a un lugar y ser siempre bienvenido en él, y sintió esa pregunta dentro de sí como si se tratara de un hambre profunda y desentrañada, todo lo cual se debe haber reflejado en su rostro porque la camarera se le acercó entonces y le dijo que no creyera las palabras lindas de Ismael porque Ismael tenía la mala costumbre de decirle palabras lindas a todas.

Momentos antes, la camarera había estado empuñando un cuchillo gigantesco, cortando limones en rodajas del otro lado del reluciente mostrador de madera del bar y haciendo que la mujer pensara en los cuchillos que ella había robado y escondido tras la visita a aquella clínica lejos de su casa en la que nadie la conocía a ella ni a su esposo. El primero con el que logró hacerse era un cuchillo de monte retráctil que, supo de verlo, no le serviría, pero que aun así guardó entre sus faldas sin ser vista. El segundo que consiguió fue un cuchillo de estilete.

—Así que esas tenemos, dos chicas hermosas, ambas en contra de un pobre e indefenso hombre —rio Ismael al ver a la camarera susurrarle algo a la mujer en la oreja, apenas perturbado por la manera en que la camarera había cercenado aquellos limones instantes antes, ni por la destreza con la que blandía el enorme cuchillo.

Cuando la camarera respondió con una mirada que lo desenmascaró como mentiroso, la mujer comprendió que eso era él, aunque no hubiese mentido sobre su familiaridad con el lugar. Aunque, bueno, ¿y qué? Ella también mintió cuando le dijo que había tenido una horrible pelea con su hermano. Cuando le dijo que había necesitado calmarse, alejarse un rato de su familia. Cuando le dijo que un vecino le hizo el favor de dejarla allí y que no fue hasta que el vecino se fue que se dio cuenta de que no tenía su billetera.

Ella veía su propio aliento al hablar—más azul mientras más mentiras decía—y tuvo miedo de que él la descubriera, de que le diera la espalda.

Pero él le dijo:

—Les sucede a todos, incluso a los mejores, como tú y yo. Estaré feliz de llevarte donde sea que vivas, cuando quieras irte.

—Te lo agradezco mucho, pero no quiero ser una molestia. En un rato puedo llamar y enseguida me vienen a buscar —dijo ella entonces, pensando en su esposo y acto seguido en sus suegros, quienes nunca venían cuando los llamaba, sin importar cuán fuerte gritara, y quienes a la mañana siguiente jamás decían palabra sobre su boca hinchada, ni sobre la sangre seca alrededor de sus fosas nasales cuando ella no tenía el valor de tocarse ni para limpiarse luego de una noche eternizada por eventos desafortunados, uno tras otro, los comerciales de sueño que su marido tomaba para recuperarse de aquellos episodios de puños, patadas y bofetones, nunca lo suficientemente largos para que ella recuperara el aliento.

Los imaginó ahora despertando en la mañana, viendo el desastre que ella había dejado antes de irse y se alegró de no tener que estar allí para verlo con ellos.

—Ninguna molestia. Es normal que las familias peleen, pero apuesto que la tuya ya está preocupada por ti —le dijo Ismael.

—Qué va. Esos seguro ya están en cama —dijo ella apretando y aflojando los dedos de los pies mientras el azul comenzaba a tornarse acero a su alrededor.

Ismael tomó un sorbo de su cerveza, mientras bebía mirándola por encima del vaso grueso de cristal escarchado grabado con la palabra "Eva's", el logo del bar.

Ella también tomó un sorbo largo, y cuando volvió a poner su vaso de cristal escarchado sobre el mostrador, vio a dos hombres armados, azules de arriba a abajo, parados a la entrada del bar, como si ella los hubiera convocado con sus mentiras.

Ismael le decía algo, pero la mujer ya no lo escuchaba, concentrada en controlar su cuerpo como ella sabía hacerlo, solo sus ojos moviéndose lentamente como si estuviera aburrida, mientras que lo que realmente hacía era buscar la salida del bar. Pero no. Estaba demasiado cerca de la entrada. Si intentaba irse en aquel momento, solo llamaría la atención.

Buscó con la vista el contenedor de metal que había estado lleno de limones, con el cuchillo grande que había usado la camarera todavía allí, casualmente inclinado hacia un lado de la vasija, y sintió desesperanza. Estaba demasiado lejos.

Tendría que inclinarse hacia el mostrador para alcanzarlo e incluso si lograra hacerlo, en nada la ayudaría. Allá en su habitación habían estado solos él y ella. Él había estado dormido ya, el cuchillo de ella era pequeño, mucho más que el de la camarera, y ella había sabido lo que tenía que hacer. No era igual con este cuchillo tan fuera de su alcance. Este cuchillo que no había descansado durante un año entre medio de sus dos colchones. Este cuchillo que no la conocía y que era demasiado ajeno para protegerla del azul que estos hombres vestían, un azul que nunca había estado de su lado antes.

No había nada que hacer excepto permanecer quieta, observando los labios de Ismael moverse como si estuviera hipnotizada por su canción, oculta a plena vista hasta que con la esquina de su ojo los vio dar la vuelta y marcharse, dos espaldas azules moviéndose en unísono hacia la puerta.

—¿Qué cosa querrían esos —dijo Ismael con un gesto de su mandíbula en dirección a los hombres de azul.

La mujer quiso decir algo, algo despreocupado, algo parecido a una broma, pero no pudo. Ella sabía que el juego había llegado a su fin. Era momento de echar a andar.

Pero ¿y si le pidiera que la llevara hasta el próximo pueblo? O tal vez no debía pedírselo, sino fingir, en vez, que quería compañía y que lo seguiría adonde fuera que él quisiera llevarla.

Extrañaba al azul que la había animado a salir de su habitación. Tomar decisiones sin su ayuda era difícil y ella no supo sino seguir sentada, mirando a Ismael y asintiendo sin escuchar palabra alguna, al tanto de que los hombres de azul regresarían y que ella tenía que estar muy lejos de allí cuando lo hicieran.

Mientras tanto, Ismael cantaba, ya no a la pantalla, sino a ella, como si sospechara que el juego estaba a punto de acabársele, su mano en la rodilla de la mujer, sus dedos cada tanto apretándosela, con ello enfureciéndola sin que ella pudiera evitarlo.

¿Qué tan malo podría ser?, le insistía ella a esa rabia que no le dejaba mentirse a sí misma, que no la dejaba descansar un poco más, con lo exhausta que estaba.

Bueno ya, pensó. Se iría con él. ¿Qué tan peligroso podría ser si todas estas personas lo conocían? Pero es que la gente también había conocido bien a su esposo. Lo conocían de la ferretería, del mercado, del bar cerca de su casa. Solo no lo conocían bien con ella.

Entonces el juego que transmitían por el televisor por fin se acabó y Ismael se inclinó hacía ella y le besó la piel debajo de su oreja justo en el momento en que comenzaban las noticias de las once, la música de apertura urgente y cada nota estridente retorciéndole los nervios.

"Buenas noches, les saluda Anna Todd y esta noche a las once: una familia es aterrorizada por un lémur salvaje y de gran tamaño, luego de que este escapara de una residencia cercana..."

Las noticias no decían nada, pese a que Anna Todd lucía un cabello azul con flequillos. Tal vez la mujer todavía tenía tiempo para distanciarse de aquellos con quienes nunca más podría vivir, incluso si esto significaba dormir en un bosque, robando ropa de tendederos, durmiendo con lémures enroscados alrededor de su cuello. Incluso si esto significaba dormir con Ismael, quien tal vez vivía lo suficientemente lejos para poder ir de ese sitio a otro, un lugar más lejano que el anterior, pensaba ella, buscando al azul por los alrededores, extrañándolo incluso más en ese momento, cuando justo necesitaba que le dijeran qué hacer para ahuyentar a aquel color acero que ya ni pretendía ser azul y se dejaba ver tan opaco como el color del cemento.

—Entonces, bella dama, ¿a dónde puedo tener el honor de llevarla? —dijo Ismael, y ella tuvo que tomar una decisión.

Él esperaba su respuesta. La miraba con ojos de perrito faldero que le recordaron a Lilly, pero también a su esposo intentando levantarse de su sueño antes de que ella pudiera agitar la cabeza para hacer que la imagen se desvaneciera. Lo vio llevar la mano hacia su propio ojo, el cuchillo hundido todavía en el punto en donde ella lo había enterrado tal y como la enfermera de la clínica le había explicado, solo para volver a caer en la cama, ya no mirándola, ni roncando, el único sonido, su regurgitar hondo, su jadeo de muerte rápida, dejándola sola con el azul de la noche y con el motor de sus propias piernas para llevarla lejos, en su mano el ojo que se había desprendido completo, limpio, sin saber por qué se lo estaba llevando.

La enfermera era apenas una niña, solo unos años mayor que la mujer. Le contó que estaba estudiando ciencias forenses y que trabajando en la pequeña clínica había visto más de lo que le era posible procesar. La mujer le dijo que ella también estaba estudiando, bueno, que estaba pensando en estudiar, quizás algo relacionado a lo que ella... y tal vez podía aprender algo de cosas forenses porque tenía mucha curiosidad sobre si era posible... si se podía... hacer esta cosa que había escuchado por ahí...

Así fue como la enfermera terminó diciéndole el tipo de cuchillo que necesitaría, algo pequeño, liviano y filudo. "La punta tiene que estar bien afilada, tanto que te corte de mirarla. Claro, ya sabes, lo digo en teoría", le había dicho mientras con delicadeza la vendaba.

Entonces le enseñó dónde enterrar el puñal, precisa y rápidamente, entre el cuello y el hombro, o justo sobre el ojo, debajo de la ceja, y cómo luego dar un tirón con fuerza, rápido, casi como si se tirara de una palanca pesada.

"Al hacerlo así, cortas la arteria subclavia y él, o ella, la persona, ya sabes, se desangraría en apenas cinco segundos. Claro que hay que recordar soltar el cuchillo de inmediato".

La mujer entendió con tanta claridad que casi se vio a sí misma siendo capaz de protegerse de todos los golpes que ella sabía pintarían de zarzamoras su futuro, y se le escapó un resuello que hizo que la enfermera pausara y frunciera el ceño como si estuviera a punto de tomar una decisión importante.

"La mayor parte de la sangre fluye hacía la cavidad torácica. Es algo relativamente limpio, creo, y ciertamente algo que vale la pena recordar si una necesita defenderse", le había dicho con la vista fija en el vendaje que le estaba asegurando.

La mujer quiso preguntarle si ella había visto a alguien hacerlo alguna vez porque no se imaginaba haciéndolo, a pesar de que estaba lo suficientemente rabiosa, herida y aterrorizada para querer poder.

Pero no preguntó y aunque pensó en ello y hasta se preparó, un año entero pasó sin que hiciera nada, lo cual explica por qué la gente del pueblo estaba tan segura de que no se le podía echar la culpa a la enfermera. ¿Cómo podrían, si ella ni siquiera había estado allí esa noche? Solo el azul había estado en la habitación, así como más tarde en el camino que llevaba al bar, y en la espuma de la cerveza, y en los ojos de perrito faldero de Ismael.

—Solo necesito un minuto para usar el baño —le dijo ahora a Ismael la mujer.

—Tómate tu tiempo. Pero no te me vayas a poner más bonita allá adentro, ¿okey?

En el baño se lavó la cara y se la secó, se limpió el pecho con toallas de papel y se arregló el cabello café oscuro sin levantar la vista por miedo a volver a ver a su marido en aquel inmenso espejo.

Usó el inodoro sin sentarse, sosteniéndose con los brazos, uno en cada lado del retrete, pese a ello orinándose los muslos y la falda, todas las bombillas fluorescentes de aquel baño fundidas menos una, y aún así ella lo vislumbró, el azul silbando desde el otro lado de la ventana sucia del baño, ahí de nuevo, llamándola, tan oscuro como siempre.

Por eso, para cuando Ismael se paró al otro lado de la puerta del baño, la mujer había tomado aire unas cien veces y se había escabullido por la puerta del extremo opuesto del pasillo oscuro.

—¿Todo bien, guapa? ¿Guapa?

Caminando rápido y sin rumbo, imaginó la voz de Ismael, su gimoteo de cachorro quejoso convirtiéndose en el ladrido de una fiera al darse cuenta de que ella se había ido, y confirmó lo que supo incluso desde que se sentó en el bar: que el azul todavía estaba dentro de ella, y que, para el azul, Ismael era el enemigo, y no tan solo un hombre, tonto y engreído en todas las maneras en las que un hombre puede serlo.

Y sin embargo, no era culpa de Ismael, pensó la mujer mientras caminaba, decidiendo que —¿por qué no?— seguiría llamándose Mayra.

Deteniéndose unos momentos detrás de un árbol, dejó que pasara una camioneta blanca y ruidosa e imaginó el momento en el que Ismael se enterara de lo que le había hecho a su esposo. Lo imaginó y deseó que él pudiera comprender algún día que ella, a él, le había hecho un favor. Que haberse ido siguiendo al azul había sido su manera de agradecerle las cervezas y la cercanía de su oído.

Aquel oído que no tenía culpa de pertenecer a un hombre criado para serlo, como ella había sido criada para ser mujer, sin que a ninguno de los dos les hubieran enseñado a compartir el poder.

Un oído humano y tibio, al cual en otro momento de su vida, ella habría estado feliz de susurrar cualquier cantidad de cosas.

BREATHE

Judah Mahay

WHY DO YOU FEAR TO BREATHE? Deliberate short breaths pinch through your mask, between lips, teeth, around the tongue, bitter, measured, never full, never willing.

The Mother's acid tears await you within reach. Her pain could be yours, a numinous plea. Shall you know her? Maybe. If this can finally awaken the dark.

"Breathe? Fear? No." The pause, a lie, lingers like cobwebs in your mind—a part of you neglected, dust strewn, dry, almost forgotten. "Ok...yes. I do...fear." The admittance stings as much as your lungs. The scarf pressing your lips, a makeshift mask, helps little. Whistle pinch of air, in, out, too slow. "Breathe." Are those words even yours? *Yes.* You agree.

The acid-tinged rain, within hand's reach, plays only a part in this dirge you call life—a penultimate of sorts. The porch's overhang, withered wood underneath, layered in metal sheets, blocks the thunderous downpour, poor protection you barely trust. Serves well enough. For the moment.

Through the ever-present twilight of an amber sky, the headlights from your red Jeep dim to yellow. Forgot to turn the engine off when you scrambled to the old farmhouse—this sky-scourge, worse than most days, came on suddenly. Barely reached your uncle's old home before the accursed rain scorched the skin—the Mother's Lament, as the Seattle academic elites liked to call it. The weatherperson referred to it as Hell's Blight, a trend that appears without end. Both fitting. That was before the radio cut out a few hours ago on the drive here. The paint from your vehicle seems to steam and sizzle, but that could just be the haze from looking through the downpour. Your ride might hold up, might not. Probably won't.

Five hours of pacing, and you still haven't kicked down the yellow-stained door to get into his house. Not sure if the color was purposeful or a product of the twisted times. Still not sure why you waited a whole hour before checking the handle. Locked. Your bastard Uncle Vic left you with this three-story ranch adjacent to a desolate corn fields converted into a defunct solar farm but never felt inclined to send a freakin' key. Not that there was anyone alive for a hundred miles who might break in. If anyone was alive at all. Another reason not to visit his damn grave at Chambers Prairie Cemetery. Your mother being buried not far from his lump of earth, just complicated things. Why not see her? You won't answer that. You can't. Not yet. *Now what?* "Not sure."

Take a breath.

"I am." A lie. You know what you mean.

Lower the scarf.

"And breathe in death's stench? I'm not looking to die."

Really? Breathe in. Savor this acrid palate.

"Maybe...why though?" How long since you've lived? Felt anything? Two, three years, maybe more? Your mother crawls into your mind again, her lofty aspirations to be a nurse and constant failures mirrored in you, whether legitimately or not, a lingering whisper lifting the hairs on the back of your neck. Vague recollections of her failures appear in your mind like a looming revenant to remind of yourself.

Being a nurse never much fit, not the nurturing type, nor much of an interest, but the firefighter exam always seemed to call to you. The call of the heat, the flex of muscle, the twitch of movement, and the desire to save, all compelled your will and your dreams, but not your actions. Too bad there isn't a need for these brave men and women anymore. Who's to save? The rats and the roaches? Rather not.

Mum never applied for nursing school either, you never took the exam. Mirror to mirror. Her death felt as sure as your own. Too soon, not even four marks of ten, taken by the tendrils of cancer from lymph node to lymph node. The infection crawled from tip to toes, till even her eyes rotted, glossed over, awaiting the decay only found in the silence of a heart. You blinked and missed the flit of her eyes and the expel of her breath, the last. The pinched release of air between still lips haunts you. Moreso than the limp uncurling of your mother's once strong hands. At least there was still people to take her body back then.

Why not you instead? Why not now? *Someone must live.* Is this living? Ignore the pain splintering your lungs. Ignore the deeper ache weighing down your legs to feet to heels, pressing your teal sneaks to the creak of the porch boards. Why didn't you wear your new hiking boots, still in the box somewhere in your abandoned flat back in Seattle a couple of hours away? Not much use now. If ever.

Doesn't matter. Today is different. *Breathe.* "Shut up!" Palms softened from cleaning too many dishes in a commercial kitchen press your temples, searching for that release of pain. *No! Seriously, listen. Just...take...a...breath. Deep to full. That's it. Pain demands reality. Now, walk away. Step off your uncle's godforsaken porch.* No! Let's be clear, this is your damn porch. Hands fall to your sides. Fingers tremble. Curl and uncurl, curl and uncurl, searching for a fist but not finding the strength. You keep your eyes keen, open, and then you do the unthinkable. You step. Wet and then heat and burn and the pain, gasping, is found. *Breathe!*

But one final horrible action remains.

In accord, you raise a trembling hand that cuts through the acid pour, steam rising from the digits like some Gorgon claw coming to claim another death, and in many ways it might. The nails seem to sizzle, this flesh that is yours. Why does it feel so distant, as if you are untethered to you? These curved fingers approach, when suddenly, with a fist-snapping grip, you tear your mask.

Released, the once protective fabric falls, caught and pressed down by rain, in an aimless descent that meets and mingles in the muck of mud that pools around your feet.

Breathe. The command softer now, somehow seems more insistent. And so you do.

The first, the second...the third, and the next. Each intake stings the throat as if dry even though you know that cannot be. From overhead, sizzling pinpricks nip at your exposed shoulders. Yet, somehow, there is piercing joy in feeling the Mother's Tears. You want to flinch. You don't. You don't deserve to. How long can your body handle this? Why did you live? Why did they not? You shrug your shoulders as if all this is normal. Not the best day for a tank top. The clouds tinted red, all too common these days.

Uncle Vic gave you this sun-sapped farmhouse. Why? You hated him. Pretty sure he hated you too, as far as you could tell. Besides your admiration for the thickness of his beard, you despised the old sot. Made sure he knew at every infrequent family gathering. The last one, what, five years ago? Couldn't be. More like seven. Called him Vic the Dick. Tried to play it off as funny but soured on it fairly quick. Loved how his face would turn red, and he would bang his fist on the table, rattling all the silverware till your mum calmed him down with her sweet voice. A crooked smile creeps into your chapped lips. Nice memory, but that's all it is and all it can be. A full year since the Tears started falling on the daily. Only seen the occasional human since and none in the past month. Only the radio lets you know others still live. Who knows where though.

You remember the arrival of his letter a week ago, descending on a cord from a hovering drone before clipping loose only to flutter at your feet. You were going to go on a walk down by Irish Lake, more of a pond, but a few ducks still roam this till waters—remnants of life. The envelope cut your forefinger as you peeled open the letter almost as if to hint at what lay within. Dictations from his will.

Kind of ironic that a drone dropped off the package. He hated tech of any kind. Preferred his pitchfork. The shock of receiving mail after weeks without any sign of human life came as a bit of a shock. At least some aspects of society still remained. The robot-automated post will probably be the last.

All these thoughts of Uncle Vic churn your stomach, and not in the good way. You snarl and spit. All that hate wells up threatening to escape your throat. Hate you still feel tingling across your skin at this very moment. Why did you come here? To burn down his home, his memory? No. The bastard is dead. Yet, your anger raises bile to crease your teeth. You lick them clean and swallow, wanting to feel the sour sear down your throat.

How could you not hate him? He let the horse farmer's son, the one who sold the meat cheap at the market stall and ground the hooves for gelatin, break in and have his way with your mum. Uncle Vic should have been there. Off getting drunk, per the usual, at the Latitude 47 Bar & Grille. He promised to watch her, after you hurried off to the big city and school. Promised you, with words stern and sounding strong, even gave you a half hug, before you zoomed off in your red Jeep.

Your mum was too pretty back then, too beautiful for this hick town of Pengue. Was. Her eyes, those amber orbs with flecks of gold never shun aftermore.

Good Ol' Uncle Vic, full of lies and failed promises, waited, leaning uncomfortably against his gray Ford pickup after your soccer game late in the semester of your sophomore year. You knew something was up. He had ice cream, half-melted. A cone for each of you, his stiff in his hand, untouched.

Mum got cancer a year later around the time they finally locked up the horse farmer's son. After the disease took her, Uncle Vic offered his sage advice. He figured your mum just stopped wanting to live after the break-in, so the first thing that came along had done her in. Uncle Vic didn't know how to parse words. Your last known relative. Still hate him, but you admit his presence helped at your mother's funeral. You wouldn't look at him even though only he attended the viewing.

Sure, you tried school again after that, but it just didn't feel right. Maybe your mum's spirit kept whispering for you to find something better, bigger. Perhaps you were catching the crazies. The note from the lawyer about Uncle Vic getting run over by his tractor didn't surprise you. The fact that his will gave you everything sure as hell did.

The downpour weakens to a dribble. The red haze of a sky, not a product of dusk nor dawn, continues spitting—the droplets of rain that reach your skin still sting. The bony knuckles of your fingers burn along with your arms, and your bared forehead drips, blurring your eyes. The dozen or so single-cord leather bracelets dangling at your wrists agitate the heat of the rain against your forearms.

The recent memory of the empty funeral parlor ebbs in and out of your thoughts before being claimed by the visceral pain of the moment—a relief of sorts.

Your tank top, once vivid azure, with the gold emblem of your soccer team, the Crescents, emblazoned on the chest, gray jeans frayed at the ankles, and teal sneakers all may be right for the heat but do little to dissuade the tumult from above. The rain falls all the more fierce. Tiny pellets fire down in an endless swath like a sick game of look at me. Your little sister Lilly, ten years younger, made up a version of that game involving toilet paper costumes. You loved her so much. When your Granny Metilda, mother's side, took her away, and they disappeared, a part of you left with her. Fragment by fragment, life splits you apart. Hopefully, she is in a better place, a better world, if that is possible.

Breathe.

"I'm trying, damn you." Who are you talking to? Yourself? You stave off the desire to step back under the porch's overhang. Something must change. Your memories have become a haunt. You are tormented by yourself, your past, and a future you cannot see. Once dry and cracked, the open field pulls you from your ranch home. Up ahead, a leafless black lotus bush plucks out of an otherwise scorched landscape. The sun bends away from zenith, beckoning. You know a lifeless land looms beyond, but you need to get away from this place. Just for a bit, to breathe.

You pass the lonely bush. It reminds you of Granddad Earl, father's side, and you don't know why nor want to. Shortish man, his twinkling brightening rooms with his always-present bowler hat do nothing to compare to the invasive black lotus shrub. Maybe because he was short, and you wanted to remember him. He told great jokes. Hopefully, he's alive somewhere in a retirement home. Probably not, but you like to dream. Or at least used to. Your mum shut him away when you first went to school in Seattle to be a botanist, since he supported the move. Probably thought you would protest. Because you would.

You stop, arms bent at your sides, hands clasped, and unfold your palms skyward. A pool of gray water gathers and spills over parted fingers with cracked skin. The sting is almost bearable, almost something you could get used to. What would it take not to remember? You cup your hands, creating a deeper divot for the rainwater to gather. Once filled to brimming, you press your lips against your wrists and arch your hands up to lick back the liquid. It stings down your throat.

That's it, breathe.

The memories leave. You are empty. The pain fills the void. Which part of your past do you hide from? Your Uncle Vic's betrayal, your mum's denial, Lilly's disappearance, Granddad Earl's absence, dropping out of school, or something else lurking outside your grasp that taints everything else? Or was it the lack of them that haunts you? Their memories are your ghosts.

You take your last gulp, and the pain ebbs a bit while still lingering with residual heat. Even so, the images, the memories, return unabated.

The ghost of Death's touch darkens your thoughts in mired memories. A cascade touching too deep into your past, each creating shockwaves that rippled along every moment that followed. Even though your uncle's death was most recent, two years ago, he died to you over a decade ago. Your mum took to the grave three years as of yesterday. She never spoke of what happened, never really spoke much at all afterward, a shell, a sin to what she used to be. Cancer made easy work of her after that. Lilly and Granddad Earl's absences feel like a death of sorts.

They are all connected in a way. Mum refused to move with you into the city and instead stay alone in the old house near Uncle Vic's farm. This house. She said she hoped her little girl would return someday and refused to lose that chance. Not sure if she spoke of Lilly or you.

You walk, and you walk, and you walk for as long as it might take. And you breathe.

Good.

How far is enough—to leave behind a pain with no etching on your skin? Have you gone crazy? Your mum was...in the end. Maybe it's genetic.

What is the worth of a life you can't live? How can you be alive if you can't see, hear, or smell what is around you? Your senses are just as numb as your soul. It's like you're stuck in a glass box that keeps clouding over no matter how much you polish the windows.

Why can't these tainted skies wash away the past? If for just a moment. Just a moment. Feel, damn you. Feel. Pain to pain. The here to the then. This reality, this pull of hair bound in a fragile fist, must mean more than the terrors of any before. What was is gone? That is done. The past, beyond the here and the now. This, this is what must be. This is what is alive. This is what should matter.

Breathe.

You try. The irony of this acid sky. The Mother's Lament. It mirrors what you desire but can't obtain. As a small child, it was so easy and almost unstoppable—the sobs, the pleas, the raw feeling. Why not now? The rain wets your eyelashes and blurs your stutter-step onward, but nothing more.

Brown puddles lap over your teal shoes, seeps and soaks. Someone should look for you. They won't. There is no one left. The city is almost barren at this point. Remember, the funeral home was empty.

You do indeed breathe and blink past the blur. You splash and slop up into the rise of what appears to be the beginning of barren plains. Endless desolation yearns beyond. Clustered strands of your black hair capture a multitude of droplets, blend, and release in large plops down your front. Some nip your pointed nose.

The world tilts, and you climb a step or two, maybe more. The water runs along fist-deep cuts in the earth parallel to your wayward path. At the peak of this not-inconsiderable slope, you lean over and ease down with a palm pressed in the mud. There is no foliage here, not even the invasive black lotus. Only wet muck. Not even the wiggle of a worm.

The mud seeps between your fingers like a warm oozing glove. You don't want to pull your hand out. The feeling hints at childhood, playing in a mud pit with Granddad Earl that he dug during one of the occasional clean rainfalls. He spent a lot of time with you after the Acid Tongue sickness took your dad. Can't really remember him. Just Granddad Earl and his twinkling smile. Back then, the mud was cool. It soothed, comforted. You could breathe easily.

How could something so simple, so instinctual, become so complicated? Breathe, you tell yourself. Just take a breath.

You curl your fingers deep, grabbing at what you do not know, feeling the tougher grit of hard dirt dig under your nails.

Beyond the farmhouse, the barn behind it, the sepia-crusted tractor, the decayed solar farm, and some twenty miles past, a harsh amber glow marks the outline of Seattle's dim cityscape, unwilling to admit defeat.

You are unsure whether your uncle's farmhouse or somewhere else will be your resting place. You will not return to that city. Let the intermittent darkness consume it. The odd job, the countless faces with nothing underneath, the words left at just that, words. Nor do you wish to be here. Where then? Your mind answers with silence.

You lay back, and the mud molds around your shoulders, gripping like hands of muck. The endless blanket of a blueless canopy overhead entreats you to accept a continuous stream of tiny pellets. The deadly rain doesn't let up, doesn't forgive—the Mother's Lament took all those around you, inflicting indiscriminately the Acid Tongue, a disease that struck Granddad Earl, sizzling in his lungs and, within days, burnt out his tongue. He was one of the lucky ones, died quickly. Yet you survived. Why? Why won't you die?

Soon, it hurts too much to stare skyward anymore. By then you really couldn't see anyway. As you close the lids of your eyes, the blur blends into a cimmerian darkness. In your mind's eye, the shadows stretch without end. Your heart slows, easing to the calm of the void.

The pain digs, tinges the core of your emptiness, infusing every pore—your body coated in pinpricks twitches. Are you coming alive or dying? Could it be both?

The memories are still there, but thankfully, as blurred as your vision. Is this catharsis? Mud and water pools warmth around your neck, soothing, massaging, freeing.

Last year back in college, before you gave up, your philosophy professor—Mr. Stein, a wide-bellied man, mustached, funny nose, too pink, too pointed, wiggled it when he smiled—once said, only when you have nothing do you have everything. Only then can you truly fathom and experience what it means to be able to reach...anything. By having something, you are tied to it. Thus, by losing it, you are freed to think further...to think beyond the constraints of that connection. Was he right? Maybe. Maybe you'll never know. Either way, you liked his mustache. Then again, you did fail his class. What would he think of you now? Of this?

Should you lay here till the pinpricks sear away your flesh, leaving the shine of bones? In a fashion that will be letting go. A part of you wants that, no longer dependent on the past. You also know, somehow, this is not true. The revenant of Death has ruled your life till now. Why let it win? Giving in to Death is not a cure...it's a termination, secession, demarcation, a narrowing to nothingness. There is no choice in nothing. The freedom you seek...resides in choices, any choice.

Mr. Stein never mentioned this. Oddly enough, your Uncle Vic did, when you still liked him, and he even convinced you to take a chance and go to college, siding with Granddad Earl. He said something akin to this in his thick drawl, while a half-chewed cigar dangled from his lips. 'If you can't do nothin' with yourself, you're just the shit, like the muck under your boot. Stuck...trampled on. Smelly. I always stink. You smell of cow shit, kid. Not right. As long as you're here, you'll be shit. This farm, the corn needs the shit. Dump loads of it. But you don't. Me, I'm just stuck to the boot of this heap. But you! Get your ass to college. Don't be the shit. It stinks. A pretty, smart lass like you don't need to be the shit. Go.'

You agreed then and still do now. *Go.* Why are you thinking of this? *Breathe.*

You lived. The acid hurts but never opened Death's door. They died. Something about you...is stronger...better made for this unforgiving world...better prepared to help those who still remain. The few. If you find them.

Lilly. Maybe out there somewhere. Playing see-me with a hat of toilet paper.

These memories jolt in flits and flashes...a chain that pits you against the present. Chains? Where are the choices in that? Muscles strain, the acid, the mud, and the pain. Is this being awake? You try to sit up, groan and strain, but the mud pulls you back into the wet earth.

Your forearms, your hands, your triceps, your shoulders, your calves, the back of your thighs, your neck, and even the tapered point at the back of your skull you never liked are held by the bitter muck.

Your heart quickens, writhing, thumping against your lung. Fear bites your lips as much as your teeth. You only wanted release. You wanted freedom. You wanted to let go. *Are you afraid?* So, you ask yourself, all too unsure. Your heart clenches as if grabbing at your ribs.

You tense, you strain, you push, you sweat.

Lilly.

The mud squirms and sucks.

Lilly.

You can't see your legs.

You grimace, feel your teeth grind in your skull, the rain patters against your pearly whites. The sting awakens.

Breathe.

You spit, you spatter, you yell, you scream. Is this what you wanted? Choices vanish, and freedom fades. You realize this path was etched in the slab of your life by you, chiseled by your actions. Your heart's response diminished, your soul peeled raw, ravaged.

Breathe and live.

With a thunderclap, lightning arcs across the blood-stained sky, a quickening arcing through your veins.

Breathe.

The acid stings. The Mother's Lament stings. But that is all. Pain simple and pure but nothing more. *I will.* All those laden memories flit away, lose their weight, feathers in the synapsis of time. The funeral hall empty. Lilly and her games of pillow tag, your mum and her empty amber eyes, Granddad Earl and his childlike spirit, and Uncle Vic and his half-melted ice cream live in you. Dead. Maybe. Maybe not. Lilly. Maybe more. The acid does not take. You smile. Then, peeling open your eyes, you breathe. The burn and the pain, but you live.

You flex your fingers and then your arms.

You clench your abs.

And you push upwards. You will not be owned by that which brought you here. Chains.

Freedom is not what you believed.

Breathe.

Life exists in moments acted upon—to be full, to bloom, thrive, humming with vibrancy, is when you act—prickle, thorns, and petals all. To act. Breathe. To be. Breathe.

Yes, breathe.

You must never react. Being free is to lead your own life. Force the next act. And the next. And the next. To be. To live. Act.

The rain falls, this acid pain of delight, and you choose. You push, you pull, you strain, you growl, you own this moment. You must...breathe. Acid air and all.

The fingers of your right hand peel free, then your palm, followed by your forearm, pivoting at the elbow, mud-slick but moving. Your head covered to your ears, the rain muffled. The rest of your body held firm, pinched at the edges. You tense your jaw and part your lips, but your lungs constrict, unyielding. You choose, you command.

Take a breath.

Take...a...breath. Breathe...*just breathe.*

Lungs fill.

Words expel.

"Lilly!

Lungs expand.

Acid...pain.

Just pain.

"I'll find you."

GOOD EVENING, MY FRIEND

Zach Keali'i Murphy

THE WEEKEND AFTER GABE GOT FIRED from the auto repair shop for accidentally causing an electrical fire, he took a Greyhound up to Albany to see his grandfather at the memory care center. The moment he'd been dreading for the past three years had finally come - his grandfather didn't recognize him anymore. "Don't take it personally," the nurse said, as if that was supposed to make him feel any less depressed about the situation.

When Gabe got home, he hopped into the shower and attempted to wash away his streak of motor oil and misery. He squeezed out a glob of shampoo, more than he intended, and it slid off his palm and splattered onto the porcelain. "Money down the drain," he thought to himself.

He tip-toed out of the bathroom and into his cramped box of an apartment. Rusty nail heads protruded from the wooden floorboards like mushrooms. Going barefoot in that place was to play a game of fate with tetanus. The stench was putrid. Mice would steal crumbs of food, and cockroaches were roommates who didn't pay rent. All the critters gave him the shivers, but he didn't have the heart to kill them.

After eating a bowl of stale cereal for dinner, Gabe crawled into his creaky bed and stared at the water-stained ceiling. His world felt a lot more empty, and his walls felt a lot more suffocating. He couldn't stop thinking about the state of his grandfather. *Maybe next time he'll know who I am*, he hoped. *Or maybe he won't. Maybe the time after that he will. Or maybe he won't.* Then Gabe began to ponder if there would even be a next time.

Just then, he heard the sound of a screech out on the balcony. He looked through the window and saw two yellowish eyes piercing the shadows. The glow of the city lights revealed a speckled coat of brown feathers and a pair of antenna-like ears that stood at attention. "An owl," he whispered. Perched upon the balcony's railing, it was the most exquisite creature he'd ever seen. Before he had the chance to exhale his halted breath, the owl flew off into the deep violet sky.

The following night, Gabe heard the screech again. His eyes widened and his heart raced as he leaped out of bed. The owl had returned to the balcony. It had its back turned to the window. "Good evening, my friend," he whispered. The owl slowly turned its head all the way around and locked eyes with him. It was a glare that was as wise as it was curious, and as calming as it was intimating. He recalled how his grandfather told him that seeing an owl means good luck. And off it went.

The owl continued to make an appearance on the balcony every night, until the night that it didn't. *Maybe tomorrow*, Gabe thought. He would stay awake until his eyelids got heavy, but the owl never showed. One day, Gabe concocted a plan to lure one of the mice from his apartment into a plastic container and use it as bait. It was his hardest, sweatiest job since he had work. When the sun set, he placed the container with the mouse in it out on the balcony and waited all night for the owl to swoop in. But the owl was nowhere to be seen. By the time the sun rose, he'd accepted that the owl wasn't coming back.

The next day, he used the remaining money from his last paycheck to purchase a Greyhound ticket and go see his grandpa up in Albany again. *Maybe when I tell him about the owl, he'll remember me*, he thought. *Or maybe he won't.*

EULOGY

Daniel R. Snyder

THE FUNERAL IS HELD in a large generation-spanning cemetery, with manicured lawns and polished granite headstones for the average, marble for the more-than-so, and pieces of nondescript rock hastily and carelessly inscribed for those who thought someone important enough for a marker, but not enough to break the bank.

...Welcome, my friends...

Jason rests peacefully in a lacquered white coffin, more ornate and of better quality than his mother can afford, and yet not as much as she feels he deserves. There is no smile on his face, and even as the mortician tried with his hands, and his family with their imaginations, they could not erase the scowl. It is the face of an eighteen year old boy who, due to circumstances he believed were beyond his control, will now be eighteen forever. A twenty-two rifle, placed in the mouth, can do that.

...There are no words, my beloved friends, to express the sorrow we feel as we say goodbye to a loved one...

His mother sits on one of the metal folding chairs lined in neat rows, the front for the immediate family and the back for friends, testing the volume of tears a tissue is capable of absorbing, as is fitting a woman grieving the loss of her son, and she looks down to the opposite end of the row of chairs, sees Jason's father, and hates.

Jason's father, sitting with the respectable amount of tears a man is allowed at such an occasion, looks at Jason's mother and does not hate. He does not judge, nor condemn, but merely pities the boy for being subjected to a convoluted and archaic legal system that decided Jason was better off with his mother, despite the fact that his mother never loved any man whose face was not on a dollar bill, spoiled him rotten, made him incapable of dealing with life, and mostly, of paramount importance, was not Catholic. It would have made all the difference.

Jason's sister now spends a larger block of her valuable time with her brother than she has in the last four years. She feels guilty about that, the unavoidable necessity of doing God's work, being the good Christian, never good enough of course, and she apologizes for that every night on her hands and knees with her hands clasped together. She didn't cry when she heard the news. She didn't cry at the viewing, and she didn't cry all the way to the cemetery. She is frightened by the joy she feels for Jason, being in that better place. She has a weak spot in her faith that allows it to bend without breaking, where she is able to convince herself that her sinful brother is in Heaven, and it comforts her like an opiate.

...Being merely human, and faulted with only human comprehension, we cannot help but be puzzled by the death of one so young. And yet, we must not question the wisdom of our Heavenly Father...

If I had only lived closer to him, his father thinks, I could have helped. I could have raised him right. He thinks this without the least sense of guilt, since it was not his fault they had gotten divorced, and not his fault the courts had not granted him custody in their paucity of moral wisdom and responsibility. The world is full of stupid people. That is not a judgment, he is careful to remind himself, since that is the Lord's job, and far be it from me to cast the first stone. It is a simple observation.

...Let us remember in hour of sorrow that we are told by the Heavenly Father that the dead in Christ shall rise again after the Tribulation and live with him forever...

His mother takes another tissue from the small black purse resting on her black clad lap, and wonders if maybe she made a mistake. Perhaps she should not have had children, or perhaps having had them, she should not have been entrusted to raise them, to bring them to the full responsibility of adulthood so they could become religious fanatics like her daughter, or decide to take a silly little twenty-two rifle that shouldn't be able to hurt anything larger than a squirrel and kill himself. That was the reward you received for giving into the old mating-birthing instinct. Be fruitful and multiply, like maggots in rotten fruit. What the hell did you expect Jason? I was too busy to date and never found you another father. Not that you ever really had one in the first place, and so I worked to give you the good life and bought you everything you ever wanted or needed and made excuses for you when you didn't want to do something, like go to school, and I gave you everything I had to give and this is what you do to thank me you ungrateful-bastard-son-of-a-bitch-just-like-your-fucking-father little idiot.

...It is not good, although often difficult to avoid, but we must try not to think overmuch on what in the future is lost. Rather, let us remember that which Jason gave us, the special joy we shared, the wonderful memories we will carry of him forever...

Look at her making a spectacle of herself, his father thinks. As if having a breakdown at the funeral will atone for all the sins she bestowed on my boy, who I had not spoken with for more than a minute or two over the last five years, justifiable, since he was so nasty to me and expected me to sympathize with him, and when I didn't, called me an asshole and hung up. Or I did, but can you blame me? Of course not. I was always willing to talk but he never listened. Not once in his life did he listen. So what can you do?

...It is often hard at these times, but we must try to avoid blaming ourselves. Jason was an intelligent boy and he made his choices, as we all do...

If my parents hadn't gotten divorced, his sister thinks, then maybe he would have been all right. If he had gone to church with me like I wanted him to. Not that Catholic stuff dad always preached. And then mom, the atheist--two opposite sides of the same worthless coin. Let them all go to hell. I tried to talk sense into every one of them and they were all so bull headed and thought that they were right all the time. If they would only have gone to church with me. Poor Jason, so afraid to live and too stupid to realize that death might be worse because he wasn't Born-Again. I don't think God will punish him for bad upbringing. Jason is in Heaven now, but if he's not, it's not my fault, and I'm not going to feel guilty about it, and it's not my job to drag them into church. Mom's mascara is running down her cheeks. She looks like a hooker and it's embarrassing to be seen even sitting by her. The least she should do is fasten another button or two on her blouse so when she sits, the world doesn't get to see that trampy black lace bra.

...It is good to see all of you here, to show your love for Jason, and support for his family. Help them as best you can, in this, their hour of need...

Jason's mother blows her nose into another of the uncounted tissues and finds that she is no longer sad. She is angry with his father for being so inattentive and not trying to help. If it's anybody's fault, it's his. I did the best that I could.

...Let us now...

Jason's father sits comfortably, knowing there was nothing he could do for Jason when he was alive, but now he can do something, which is make sure Jason gets Last Rites, and go home and pray and pray and pray and get priests to pray until God takes mercy on Jason's soul and lets him into Heaven. I did not fail as a father. He failed as a son, and his mother failed us both.

...Bow our heads...

I did everything I could, his sister thinks, and there was nothing I could do to help him because he wasn't willing to help himself. I offered to take him to church. If mom and dad hadn't always been at each other's throats. If we could have all gone to church as a family.

...In silent prayer...

And so the sermon ends and the prayer is indeed silent. The white lid is closed and the few guests in attendance quickly file away. For a long while, Jason's mother, father, and sister simply stare at each other, uncertain of what to do next, and then slowly come together and embrace. They do not meet each other's eyes, nor do they speak, but merely hold each other, finding comfort not in the embrace of family, but in knowing there is someone else to blame.

EL DIABLO ME ESCUCHÓ

Olga Isabel Castilla Rocha

"OJO CON DECIR LO QUE QUIERES en voz alta, mija, que el diablo escucha aun sin tener orejas", dice una señora que pasa frente a tu casa todas las mañanas, sin falta, después de que canta el gallo de tus vecinos. Cierras tus ojos pesados, lagañosos, y los abres antes de que se vuelvan a dormir. *¿Cómo sabe que el diablo no tiene orejas?*, piensas antes de ver el reloj. Son las 4 de la mañana: es la misma hora a la que te despertaste ayer y anteayer. Y te despierta lo mismo de siempre: un sueño con el diablo. Al menos no sueñas con ese diablo estereotípico que te mostraron de pequeña, pero extrañamente sabes que es él, aun cuando se viste de traje o solo aparezca con un bañador. Es un sueño que controlas al principio y en el que haces lo que se te da la gana, haces lo que en el mundo real nunca haría una persona normal. Y tú misma sabes que te hace falta eso que haces en tus sueños, aunque lo niegues; te hace falta no estar sola. Por eso fantaseas con abrazar al que se sienta a tu lado en tus clases y te espantas cuando a veces vas más lejos y te imaginas desnuda con ese que te roza el brazo cuando pasa. Te preguntas si estás loca o si eres rara, mas la soledad en la que te tienes le da una respuesta obvia a esa pregunta. *Tal vez por eso no descanso en esos malditos sueños*, piensas. Vuelves a maldecir tus sueños como si en realidad te disgustaran, y ocultas cómo te encantan esos labios que nunca has besado, esas manos que nunca has agarrado, ese cuerpo con el que nunca has estado... Todo eso te gusta. Lo sabes bien. Pero ya estás cansada de las madrugadas. Te harta tocarle la puerta al sol antes de que salga. En el espejo tus ojeras parecen dos colchones de agua; tus labios, orugas negras; tus ojos, dos luces apagadas. Pasas tus manos por tu cabello y agarras tu cabeza con rabia, porque estás exhausta. Es como si en tus sueños vivieras otra vida que no te deja vivir ahora.

"Mija, yo creo que es el demonio el que te tiene así, tan flaquita y sola", dice la señora de las mañanas luego de que le contaras sobre tus sueños. ¿Que por qué le contaste? Ni tu misma sabes. Solo sabes que necesitabas hablar con alguien, con quien fuera. Y a pesar de haberla criticado ayer, ahora sí quieres escucharla; porque quizá, según tú, pueda haber algo de razón en esas palabras que ya estaban enmudecidas y eran solo aire en tu mente.

"Pocos te dirán lo que yo te digo ahora, mujer: el diablo, aunque es diablo, es de amores, y te lo digo por experiencia. Pero no te preocupes, que ya luego de un tiempo encuentra a otra persona más sola que tú. Así lo seducen sin saberlo, con la soledad". Tus ojos se abren y ante ellos se muestran los recuerdos de esos sueños oscuros y tentadores. Ahora todo comienza a tener sentido para ti. *Besé al diablo*, gritas pensando. *Besé y toqué al diablo.* Dejas a la señora y corres a tu cuarto. Vuelves a recordar esos sueños que una vez viste como inocentes y otras veces como depravados. Te es imposible negar la felicidad que te dieron muchos de ellos, pero también te es imposible negar lo reales que se sentían todos. Tu mente parece no cesar de conversar consigo misma, hasta que la noche cae y la sombra de la luna arropa tu cama. Escuchas el silencio por tu ventana y miras el techo para evitar cerrar tus ojos. No quieres volver a soñar, supongo. Arrugas tus párpados y luchas contra el sueño. Yo, como todo un caballero, te acaricio sin que te des cuenta. Te tapo la boca sin que me veas. Ahora, como si me sintieras, te preguntas por qué te visito... por qué te visto con mi piel. Y te respondo susurrándote al oído, recordándote que fue tu voz la que me llamó esa vez que dijiste que no querías estar sola. Creo que me sentiste: los vellos de tus brazos me lo dicen todo. Ahora, por fin, te preguntas por la voz que estás escuchando y que sigue hablándote; ya sabes quién es el que habla. El diablo te escuchó.

CRÍTICA

THE POETICS OF DIFFERENCE AND THE POLITICS OF REPETITION IN *LA CASA DE BERNARDA ALBA*

Wifredo de Ràfols

WHEN FEDERICO GARCÍA LORCA finished writing *La casa de Bernarda Alba* in June 1936, he could scarcely have known it was to be his last play. Even if only as cold comfort, it may have pleased him to know what became of the drama he never lived to see produced. His final major work would not only survive his murder and outlive a protracted Francoist suppression of the arts that would ban it from being staged in Spain for nearly thirty years, it would also begin to thrive on world stages within a decade after his death. Its various productions, beginning in Buenos Aires in March of 1945 and continuing thereafter on a global trajectory from San Francisco to London and beyond, would deliver it from obscurity and secure its place among classics of world literature. The play's scathing censure of authoritarian suppression could not be suppressed. On the contrary, in the eighty-five years since its creation, *La casa de Bernarda Alba* has been performed in theaters worldwide, adapted for film and television, transformed into ballets, operas, and musicals, reprinted in textbooks, anthologies, and critical editions, and translated into languages ranging from Afrikaans to Urdu. It has also been analyzed by countless critics, many of whom laud it as a masterpiece and find it to be comparable with the works of a wide array of authors and producers, from Pérez

Galdós and García Márquez to Sophocles and Spielberg.[1]

Most critics would agree that the play's staying power is attributable to its vivid dramatic and poetic language, to the universality of its themes and characters, and to what it says about human nature in general and 1920s Andalusian culture in particular. In this essay I propose a reading that may shed additional light on Lorca's achievement. While the dialectic between autocracy and rebellion has been studied by many Lorca scholars, it has not been fully fleshed out. Doing so by viewing it through the deceptively simple lenses of difference and repetition yields new insights into the play's structure and more accurately accounts for its durability and its relevance to the push and pull between autocracy and democracy the world continues to face to this day.

In analyzing the degree to which the play is made up of a tightly woven fabric of a dozen motifs, I argue that the forces of difference and repetition associated with those motifs are expressed as cultural representations of rebellion and despotism, with one force promoting conduct that threatens to upend the established order while the other seeks to preserve it. [2] Aesthetically, the effective appearance, disappearance, and reappearance of motifs and the interplay between them is, in Gilles Deleuze's words, "the highest object of art" and constitutes the "ultimate theatre" (293). While examining instances of difference and repetition is useful in appraising artistic merit, it also opens a pathway to a deeper understanding of the cultural dynamics that underpin the play. In this respect, questions of difference and

---

[1] Among critics relating Lorca's play with other works: on Pérez Galdós's *Doña Perfecta*, see Thomas Blake "Maternity," Linda C. Fox, and Jaroslav Rosendofsky; on Eugene O'Neill's *Desire Under the Elms*, see Emilio José Álvarez Castaño; on feminine characters in works by Gabriel García Márquez, see Cabello Pino; on Tennessee Williams's *Suddenly, Last Summer*, see José I. Badenes; on Alfonso Sastre's *Escuadra hacia la muerte*, see Mary Rice; on Steven Spielberg's *Schindler's List*, see María Teresa García-Abad García; on Sophocles's *Antigone* and T. S. Elliot's *The Wasteland*, see Christina Dokou; on Anton Chekhov's *Three Sisters*, see Michel Frucht Levy; on Rojas's *La Celestina*, see Eduardo Galán Font.

[2] Invoking the fabric metaphor (textile > text) is not unusual, nor is the weaving trope foreign to Lorca, who summons it in this play (62, 85) and more conspicuously in *Mariana Pineda*; *Doña Rosita, la soltera*; and "La monja gitana." Most critics invoke fewer and broader threads than I do here; Salvatore J. Poeta, for example, speaks of "the play's triple thematic thread of its economic, social, and moral/religious motifs" (741).

repetition pertain not to iterations of a motif but, more importantly, to whether and how we associate it with promoting change (difference) or preserving the status quo (repetition). As I hope to show, in *La casa de Bernarda Alba* the youngest of the five daughters, Adela, and her grandmother, María Josefa, to the exclusion of other characters, are repeatedly associated with nature and its creative force, while the perpetuator of Spanish patriarchal society, Bernarda, and those under her sway are repeatedly associated with resisting change, shunning nature's creative force, and abiding by established norms.

Extrapolating from the microcosm of the theater to a broader sociopolitical context, Adela, María Josefa, and the power of nature embody what Deleuze calls "the poet," who "speaks in the name of a creative power, capable of overturning all orders and representations in order to affirm Difference" (53). Although several of María Josefa's surrealist rants are indeed poetic, "poet" here serves as a catch-all intended to personify the forces of difference and rebellion. For the gay spectator who senses Lorca is writing from the closet, "poet" includes not just the aforementioned actors but the author himself, who in this and much of his work sought to affirm difference. But here Lorca does not simply write from the closet and against it. He also writes from and against the room where María Josefa is locked up, from and against the despot's prison house, and from and against the very fabric of society that condemns difference and exalts the repetition of mores and norms. Opposing the will of the poet, Bernarda embodies "the politician," who is "above all concerned with denying that which 'differs' so as to conserve or prolong an established historical order" (Deleuze 53). Bernarda holds no political office, but in a striking number of ways her traits and conduct otherwise befit the epithet of "politician," intended to personify the force of repetition and the will to hold on to power by perpetuating conventional norms.

In dramatizing a domestic struggle between rebellion and despotism, Lorca was attuned to how difference and repetition compete not only in the aesthetic realm but also in the sociopolitical one. That competition continues to play out in society to this day (for example, Donald Trump's slogan, "Make America Great Again," is a call to repeat or return to the past, while Barak Obama's "Hope and Change" is a forward-looking call to enact difference). As a cultural representation of this dialectic, *La casa de Bernarda Alba* is an object lesson on Spain's efforts to resist modernity in the early part of the twentieth century, a representation dictators would as soon ban, for, despite the play's gendered setting—a provincial home in which a woman instead of a man upholds patriarchal discourse—it shows that the result of thwarting difference, stifling individuality, silencing opposition, promoting rote thinking, and autocratically enforcing edicts designed to conserve power and to prolong established hierarchical discourse is death. In this last respect, the play's tragic outcome, the death of Adela and the end of rebellion, is likewise consonant with Deleuze's schema, in which death represents "the cancellation of difference" (259).

I use the term "poetics" here not so much in opposition to hermeneutics as in concert with the notion of discovering how structural elements in the text—in this case, those associated with difference—operate, accepting also the term's longstanding connotative linkage with poetry and, thereby, the aforementioned Deleuzian "poet." I use the term "politics" to refer to activities associated with the governance of a nation and, in particular, to those associated with autocratic regimes, but which here apply analogically to the governance of a household and which, given the extent to which they advance repetition and are spearheaded by an autocrat, I link with the aforementioned Deleuzian "politician." (I also understand that one could as easily speak of the politics of difference or the poetics of repetition, but since in this play the bulk of political maneuvering implicates repetition and the bulk of poetic subversion implicates difference, the poetics of difference and the politics of repetition will be the polestars of this essay.)

When the curtain opens, a prescribed silence broken by a funeral toll foreshadows that Deleuzian cancelation that signifies death. The toll marks the death of Bernarda's second husband, Antonio María Benavides—the first topic to be taken up on stage (49–50). Death and silence, which coalesce by their very nature and their repeated juxtapositions in the play (on the intimate connection between them, see Dru Dougherty 93) make their last joint appearance just before final curtain, when Bernarda, learning her daughter Adela is dead, calls for a funeral toll and issues her last command, "¡Silencio!" (151). Thus, the play opens by invoking silence, a funeral toll, and death, and closes by invoking death, a funeral toll, and silence. This palindromic symmetry, reminiscent of poetic closure, creates a selvage of emptiness and anguish that captures the stifling consequences of oppression. While opening with the death of Bernarda's second husband, itself a repetition of the death of the first, signals the demise of the patriarch, it only makes way for a gynarchy whose ideology is unmistakably patriarchal. Once established at the outset, the subject of death recurs throughout, not only as it relates to the passing of Bernarda's father, daughter, and first and second husbands, but also as a foreboding note that is frequently struck in the dialog. The recent death of Benavides gives rise to the topic in expected ways—for example, in repeated mentions of "luto" and the color black (on the use of black and white, see Luis Fernández Cifuentes 77). But the motif also serves as a ready-made intensifier that lends gravity to remarks about sundry matters, as when Poncia says of Bernarda, "Es capaz de sentarse encima de tu corazón y ver cómo te mueres durante un año," a succinct allegory that conveys both the will to oppress and the effect of oppression (51). Instantiations of the theme eventually culminate in Adela's death, but not before connecting with the house-as-prison motif when Adela portrays the house itself as a place of death: "He visto la muerte debajo de estos techos y he salido a buscar lo que era mío" (144). As we will see, the morbid atmosphere that permeates the household is due not merely to frequent references to death but, more insidiously, to a repressive climate in which repetition trumps difference and in which any conduct that strays from the norm is taboo.

Silence, from the start associated with death, frames both the play and Bernarda's discourse, which opens with "¡Silencio!" and closes with the same utterance (56, 151). The thread reappears often, with sixteen direct mentions of "silencio." Breaks in the dialog and the many instances in which characters tell each other to shut up (for instance, "calla esa lengua atormentadora" [69]) suggest that the dynamics of silencing are well established in the Alba household, where on one occasion a maid muzzles María Josefa with a sack (63). As Bilha Blum notes, "choosing to silence whatever social or behavioral issues are silenced by cultural norms [...] the artist can thus intentionally point to them" (46). Censorship and silencing opposition, the stock-and-trade of despots, comes second nature to Bernarda, who at every turn snuffs out individuality and any deviation from normative behavior. Characters often suppress their own speech. For example, Adela's reaction on learning that Angustias is betrothed to Pepe is truncated by ellipsis—"Pero Pepe el Romano..."—and when the crucial discrepancy between the predawn hour Pepe reportedly left the house comes to light, Martirio's reaction is simply, "Entonces...," (77, 117). Bernarda's approach to that discrepancy is likewise inscrutable, showing concern for neither Angustias nor the truth, but only for what people might say about it and, consequently, for keeping silent on the subject: "No se hable de este asunto" (118).

While the dialog is peppered with a modicum of outright lies, hypocrisy is the more pervasive recourse for abiding by Bernarda's tenets, just as it is for minions and enablers who either keep silent or parrot the views of their autocratic leaders, venting their dissent only in private. To cope with having to seem loyal while concealing true feelings, playacting is a logical stratagem, one that is first enacted by a servant before any main character enters. As the funeral bells toll, she takes to cursing the deceased: "¡Fastídiate! ¡Ya no volverás a levantarme las enaguas detrás de la puerta de tu corral!" (This is the first of many instances in which the corral is associated with sexuality.) When mourners from the service enter, this same servant turns on a dime and breaks into histrionic wailing: "¡Ay Antonio María Benavides ...! Yo fui la que más te quiso de las que te sirvieron" (55). Audiences can hardly fail to notice this blatant display of hypocrisy. Once introduced, the thread reappears in subsequent scenes as a barely discernible but growing undercurrent of pretense in which every character, save María Josefa, participates. Adela and Martirio contribute much duplicitous talk meant to conceal their true feelings for Pepe, until in a flurry of internecine sniping they disclose them to one another in the final Act. This is not to say there are no hints of hypocrisy or explicit mentions of it along the way, as when Magdalena tells Martirio, "¡Nunca he podido resistir tu hipocresía!" (76). While the contentious issue of Pepe accounts for much hypocritical behavior, there is a broader sense in which everyone must behave that way. After all, abiding by the social norms and cultural traditions the despot imposes requires the kind of sustained suppression of natural human inclinations one might find in a convent, where routine and repetition rule the day and difference is shunned. This explains why, for example,

Poncia, who in truth would be spitting on Bernarda "un año entero" if she could, is instead her enabler, chief of staff, and docile servant—in her words, a "buena perra" (52)—but it does not explain how Bernarda herself comes to be a hypocrite. For that we must turn to one of her obsessions, her concern for what "las gentes del pueblo" might say about her (118). Her keen interest in managing public opinion, typical of politicians, will be discussed shortly. For now, let her reaction to the death of Adela serve as an emblematic example of hypocrisy. Even though she has every reason to believe Adela had sexual relations with Pepe, instead of expressing grief upon learning of her suicide, foremost on her mind is making sure everyone knows her youngest died a virgin. Her exact words bear the earmarks of a press release in which, to reinforce self-promotion, she refers to herself in the third person: "Ella, la hija menor de Bernarda Alba, ha muerto virgen" (151). Here and elsewhere, hypocrisy is at the service of repeating and preserving what is proper and canceling that which differs. If the household is to maintain its façade of propriety and the despot is to safeguard her social standing in the community, proclaiming virtue where none exists, a hallmark of hypocrisy, is a must.

For Bernarda, managing public opinion means broadcasting her decency and making sure the Alba reputation remains unsullied. Her obsessive preoccupation with being perceived as the head of a family that abides by the conventions of bourgeois Spanish society is hinted at early on, when Poncia refers to her derisively as "ella, la más decente" (51). "Decente" and "decencia" are subsequently mentioned often, as in this remark, in which the despot inadvertently captures the struggle between the forces of nature and tradition: "¡Cuánto hay que sufrir y luchar para hacer que las personas sean decentes y no tiren al monte demasiado!" (68). Martirio accuses Adela of not being a "mujer honrada," while Angustias physically restrains Adela, saying, "¡Ladrona! ¡deshonra de nuestra casa!" (144, 149).[3] Perhaps the most poignant example of invoking the sanctity of decency, in this case to exact punishment on a transgressor, occurs at the end of Act II, when news arrives that Librada's daughter has had a child out of wedlock and

[3] Closely related to decency and reputation, the topic of honor is taken up in several studies, including Eduardo Urbina's "De Calderón a Lorca: El tema del honor en *La casa de Bernarda Alba*."

killed it for fear of being ostracized. Before calling for hot coals to be placed on the site of this woman's sin and exclaiming, "¡Matadla! ¡Matadla!," Bernarda gives her justification for the punishment: "que pague la que pisotea su decencia" (121). The politician holds decency, or appropriateness to and repetition of the standards of society, in such high regard that indecency is a crime punishable by death.

Bernarda's preoccupation with decency goes hand in hand with her concern for what the neighbors think. This concern with public opinion is often explicit, as when she fears the neighbors will catch sight of her mother in the courtyard (64). Decency, reputation, and related threads often appear tightly braided. Note, in the following example, how she connects silence and reputation: "¿Qué escándalo es éste en mi casa y con el silencio del peso del calor? Estarán las vecinas con el oído pegado a los tabiques" (107). In this next example, death, decency, tradition, and class distinctions (the latter two will be taken up shortly) are so tightly bound that they are hardly distinguishable: "¿Es decente que una mujer de tu clase vaya con el anzuelo detrás de un hombre el día de la misa de su padre?" (65). The daughters are well aware of the mandate to keep up appearances, even as they lament its effect on them. Magdalena puts it in a nutshell: "nos pudrimos por el qué dirán" (73). Her mother's insistence on preserving the Alba reputation is indeed corrosive and, in the end, lethal. It is also consistent with the ethos of an autocratic politician for whom optics and public opinion matter more than facts or the truth.

When combined with the despot's classism and her penchant for hewing to tradition, these preoccupations with how others view the Albas transforms the house into a veritable prison. The house-as-prison motif has several variants, including references to the house as a "convento" and "presidio" (99, 148), as well as numerous mentions of the "paredes," "tabiques," "muros," "techos," and "tejas" that keep the daughters confined.[4] The message of confinement is clear from the start, when the despot decrees an eight-year period of mourning and adds, "Haceros cuenta que hemos tapiado con ladrillos puertas y

[4] "Casa" is the most frequent common noun in the play (one of the many features it shares with Galdós's *Doña Perfecta*—see Fox 57–65). On various meanings of the spaces and layout of the house, see Fernández Cifuentes (79–81); on interior and exterior spaces as they relate to gender, see John P. Gabriele (381–92).

ventanas" (62). (A contrastive repetition of "puertas y ventanas" occurs in Act II, when the harvesters are heard singing in the distance, "Abrir puertas y ventanas / las que vivís en el pueblo" and Martirio repeats the refrain [102].)[5] The five chains Bernarda wields to restrain her daughters and the bricks with which she walls up doors and windows may be figurative, but their effect is real (62, 111). One of the methods she uses to ensure her figurative language takes on literal meaning is to create a constant state of surveillance, which she describes in various ways: "Nací para tener los ojos abiertos. Ahora vigilaré sin cerrarlos ya hasta que me muera"; "¡Aquí no se vuelve a dar un paso que yo no sienta!"; "Mi vigilancia lo puede todo"; "A la vigilia de mis ojos se debe esto" (118, 119, 136, 137). In consequence of this vigilance, reminiscent of mass surveillance in a police state, her subjects have not only internalized her edicts but also what Mac E. Barrick calls her "evil eye," which they believe is always on the alert for any noncompliance (472). This visibility effect is akin to the panopticon effect Michel Foucault describes in *Discipline and Punish*. As with convicts in a panopticon prison, Bernarda has induced in her subjects "a state of conscious and permanent visibility that assures the automatic functioning of [her] power" (Foucault 203). Cloistered in a house where they have accepted the notion that any move they make is subject to detection, the daughters are socially and sexually stifled, rendered housebound (or closeted) to the point that to go for a walk the only outlet is to walk from room to room—"Vengo de correr las cámaras. Por andar un poco"—much as inmates do in an exercise yard (73). The house thus becomes a locus of repression, a restrictive space that forbids difference and fosters repetitive behavior.

Bernarda's classism contributes in no small measure to keeping her subjects confined. Bantering with a maid, Poncia gives the first hint of the despot's wealth when she lets it be known that "mis hijos trabajan en sus tierras" (52). The maids are well aware of their landless status and are not indisposed to characterizing it, as when one of them refers to burial plots as "la única tierra que nos dejan a las que no tenemos

[5] Onstage remarks about offstage events are fraught with sexual innuendo, or what Adela calls "asuntos de hombres y mujeres" (96). From the harvesters' song to gossip about Adelaida's father's wives to what Poncia reports Paca la Roseta did—"Dicen que iba con los pechos fuera"—what occurs beyond the confines of the house underscores what must never occur within it (67).

nada" (53). After shooing away a beggar who came by the house for scraps, this same maid refers to her own class as "las que vivimos en las chozas de tierra" (53). Once the disparity between rich and poor is established, Bernarda enters, scolds the maid, and minces no words when expressing how she feels about the poor: "Los pobres son como los animales. Parece como si estuvieran hechos de otras sustancias" (56). As Dougherty points out, the oppressed in this drama include anyone who works for a living (94). In that regard, note how Bernarda blends her fondness for ordering silence with her views on the lot of the working class: "Obrar y callar a todo. Es la obligación de los que viven a sueldo" (115). Class-conscious to a fault, Bernarda has raised her daughters accordingly. Martirio and Magdalena, for example, accept that they cannot go out to the fields and mingle with the harvesters because "¡Cada clase tiene que hacer lo suyo!" (100). Keeping within the bounds of their social class brings with it the dubious privilege of staying home and not engaging with townsfolk, which in turn ensures their spinsterhood. The politician explains to Poncia that none of her daughters has ever had a beau because "Los hombres de aquí no son de su clase" (68). A case in point is Martirio's tryst with Enrique Humanes, who, we learn in Act I, never showed up at the appointed hour. Not until well into Act II do we learn that Bernarda sabotaged her daughter's date with the suitor because his father was a mere field hand (113). When Poncia implies that such measures have led to the current state of affairs, the despot puts her in her place, reminding her that she is of low birth. Preserving class distinctions, a predilection of the ruling class, includes transmitting "an established historical order" across generations through proper spousal selection, an objective the despot pursues with little regard for the harm it does to her daughters (Deleuze 53).

Marrying within one's social class is a time-honored tradition, one of many Bernarda upholds. The motif of tradition comprises the social, religious, and family customs that characterize Andalusian culture and that are always at play and often foregrounded in this drama. Since the concept encompasses a wide gamut of human behavior, instances of its varied manifestations—from the ritual prayers repeated at the outset to the superstitions voiced by several characters (inventoried by Barrick 469–77)—are too numerous to review here. Suffice it to say that Bernarda is the main proponent and enforcer of tradition and that she readily invokes social, religious, and family customs to suit her needs. While she frequently issues incidental admonishments based on social mores—for example, "A tu edad no se habla delante de las personas mayores" (56)—she also mandates what amounts to her daughters' house arrest, an order she justifies by invoking a conflation of traditions. The excessive period of mourning she decrees is years longer than the period prescribed by catholic doctrine, an escalation derived from comingling a religious tradition with a family one: "Así pasó en casa de mi padre y en casa de mi abuelo" (62). The despot's unquestioning devotion to these and many other established norms breeds rote thinking and, ultimately, not thinking at all—in her words, "No pienso ... Yo ordeno" [112])—with the result that free will, difference, and individuality are snuffed.

Pitted against tradition, the force of nature represents the only contrarian thread in a fabric of complementary elements, all of them associated with repetition and the Deleuzian politician. While nature's biological dynamism can be said to involve both repetition and difference—the former in replication, the latter in the adaptive trait variances that drive evolution—its function in the play falls on the side of difference and serves to contrast the wild with the civilized, natural law with moral law, and instinctual appetites with disciplined restraint. The nature motif is carried forward primarily by Adela and, to a lesser extent, María Josefa, whose surrealist rants, peppered with lyricism and mentions of flora and fauna, espouse difference, desire, and rebelliousness. Locked in a veritable prison within a prison, María Josefa is doubly confined and, whenever she manages to escape from her room, poetically candid in her fanciful harangues. While according to her all of the daughters are in love with Pepe, Adela is the one whose desire burns too hot to be contained. In this regard, Juan Godoy posits that "one of the central tenets of heterosexual ideology is that a man ought to be [...] the one who looks rather than the one who is looked at, the one who desires rather than the one desired" (105). While Godoy makes a strong case for how Lorca reverses that tenet by depicting Pepe as the object of desire (106), and while it is true that the bulk of textual evidence points to the daughters desiring Pepe rather than vice versa, it is also true that we can only know of his desire circumstantially, since he never appears on stage. But desire Adela he must, or he would never have come calling at her window, where she intentionally makes herself into an object of desire by posing half naked with the light on to attract his male gaze (Adela is prone to objectifying her body, saying, for example, "¡Yo hago con mi cuerpo lo que me parece!" [93, 95]). Endeavoring to explain herself and to shirk responsibility for her actions, Adela, whose name alludes to her being the one who "se adelanta" (119, 144), portrays her desire as an irresistible force of nature, likening it to a fire in her loins—"por encima de mi madre saltaría para apagarme este fuego que tengo levantado por piernas y boca" (96). In Ricardo Doménech's view, "su relación con Pepe el Romano es de lo más *natural*" (193, emphasis in the original). A menagerie of fauna, including a lamb, a wolf, a lion, untamed mules, and tongueless frogs, carries forward the nature thread, often dispersing and decentering it from its core mission: to depict Adela's repressed sexual desire as an unstoppable force of nature that threatens to upend the Alba household. Sometimes faunal images are directly centered on that mission, as when she likens herself to a hare, too fast for Poncia's clutches, and Pepe to a lion who "dominará toda esta casa" (96, 149). Among the many reappearances of the thread, a telling example of the conflict between it and the house-as-prison motif occurs while the politician chats with her friend Prudencia, and an untamed stallion is heard to buck against the stall—the corral having been established as a locus of nature and sexuality. The pent-up stallion, a symbol of virility, threatens to bring down the house, even as Pepe and what Adela feels for him threaten to do the same.[6] Ironically, Bernarda elaborates on this possibility, apparently oblivious to the symbolism contained in her words. Referring to "El caballo garañón, que está encerrado y da coces contra el muro," she says, "Pues encerrad las potras en la cuadra, pero dejadlo libre, no sea que nos eche abajo las paredes" (126). No great leap of imagination is required to associate "las potras" with the daughters, "las paredes" with the house-as-prison, and "el caballo" with Pepe and the force of nature. Unlike her sisters, Adela's attention is often fixed on natural phenomena—including the stars, comets, lightning bolts—as representations of the power of nature. "Tiene el cielo unas estrellas como puños," she says;

[6] In Barrick's view, the white stallion represents "fertility and death" (474). Manuel Antonio Arango notes that "El caballo es un símbolo de la impetuosidad del deseo animal del hombre ... cuyo valor es eminentemente sexual" (174). Doménech offers insightful interpretations of the stallion, as well as of dogs, the lamb, the sun, the moon, water, and the vegetable kingdom (198–207).

then, raising the subject of comets and lightning bolts, she expresses her appreciation of disruptions to the status quo: “me gusta ver correr lleno de lumbre lo que está quieto y quieto años enteros” (132–33). Whether we view her celestial observations as trite or portentous of rebellion, when juxtaposed with Amelia and Martirio’s reaction to them—“Yo cierro los ojos para no verlas” and “A mí las cosas de tejas arriba no me importan nada” (133)—the contrast is clear: Adela is captivated by the power of nature, while her sisters are not. In keeping with her discourse of non-thinking, Bernarda adds, “es mejor no pensar en [esas cossas]” (133).

The notion that marrying for money is unnatural only exacerbates matters.[7] When Poncia, aware of the “tormenta” brewing in every one of the daughters’ rooms, tells Bernarda who Pepe’s actual lover is, she speaks of the true inclination “de las cosas” (115–16). If nature had its way, that inclination would be for Pepe to wed the youngest; according to Poncia, even the air agrees that Pepe marrying the oldest is wrong (116). By this point, the unruly thread of nature is inextricably entangled in the fabric of the mutually complementary threads that compete against it, chief among them tradition and the politician’s despotism. As the action builds to a climax, Adela increasingly shows herself to be different from all those who abide by established norms. Functioning as the poet in Deleuze’s schema, she, her grandmother, and the force of nature are subtly drawn representations of a mounting mutiny that abandons all pretense in the final scene, when Adela breaks the despot’s scepter in two, declaring that she is no longer under her mother’s spell and answers only to the man she likens to a lion (148-49). In a faunal menagerie in which María Josefa characterizes Bernarda as a leopard, Magdalena as a hyena, and the daughters as tongueless frogs, it stands to reason that Adela would trump them all by likening her lover to the king of beasts.

Before turning to Bernarda’s despotism, it is worth remembering that in this “drama de mujeres” in which gender differences are starkly drawn, social and religious conventions have cemented those

[7] Lorca’s distaste for arranged marriages and marriage itself as an artificial social construct is also evident in *Bodas de sangre*, in which, much as Adela does, the Novia exclaims, “¡Ay ... qué fuego me sube por la cabeza!” and Leonardo blames his infidelity on nature: “Que yo no tengo la culpa, que la culpa es de la tierra” (156).

differences into rigid stereotypes that keep men and women worlds apart. Gender stereotyping comes into play soon after Bernarda enters, when she cuts short gossip about which men attended the funeral service: "Las mujeres en la iglesia no deben mirar más hombre que al oficiante, y a ése porque tiene faldas" (58). In the next scene, Magdalena complains that she would rather do anything than stay home all day, to which her mother remarks, "Eso tiene ser mujer" (63). While this formula gives the politician yet another justification for keeping her subjects confined, her classist discourse in turn justifies gender stereotyping: "Hilo y aguja para las hembras. Látigo y mula para el varón. Eso tiene la gente que nace con posibles" (63). This birthright, which should bring with it upscale advantages, when combined with another accident of birth—being born a woman—only brings seclusion and the repetitive conduct that goes with it. Amelia puts it this way: "Nacer mujer es el mayor castigo" (101). Male roles are likewise stereotyped, even if no man appears on stage. Thus, a murdering philanderer is not in jail because men cover up for each other, married men soon abandon their conjugal duties, and men frequent prostitutes because "los hombres necesitan estas cosas" (71, 91, 101). (Robert Lima inventories the "invisible males" mentioned in the play [136–47]]). Yet, according to Poncia, keeping men and women apart is what accounts for the daughters' woes: "Son mujeres sin hombre, nada más" (119). Even though Angustias is about to marry and therefore about to bridge the divide, the counsel her mother gives her serves instead to perpetuate it, since women should not speak to men unless spoken to—"Y cuando te cases, menos" (131). After rearing its head often, gender stereotyping makes a final appearance at the end of the play, when the despot, having tried to shoot Pepe and missed, blames her bad aim on her gender: "No fue culpa mía. Una mujer no sabe apuntar" (151).

Bernarda's despotism is a governing theme and arguably the leitmotif of the play. Rather than offer an extensive analysis of a thread we have already seen interweave with most of the threads discussed earlier, what follows is a brief account of how it is brought into prominence by repetition and, more importantly, how it functions to promote repetition itself by denying "that which 'differs'" (Deleuze 53). Like many women high in social dominance orientation (see the data-driven study by Helena R. M. Radke et al.), Bernarda feels empowered rather than restricted by the patriarchal values she espouses, likely because she believes they are God-given and good, and not a social construct devised by men in furtherance of their own ends. Her dominance is made known even before she enters, when, at the mention of her name, Poncia lets loose with two epithets, "¡Mandona! ¡Dominanta!" (50). Later, she will also be called "tirana" and "dominadora" (51, 148). As if to ratify these characterizations, the moment she enters she begins issuing commands and chastises the maid for not having cleaned well enough.[8] Her political legitimacy is derived from the demise of the authoritarian father figure, which leaves a vacuum that is automatically filled by the authoritarian mother figure. Since there are no longer any men in the house to challenge her, Bernarda is free to act as the martinetish guardian of decency, tradition, class distinctions, gender stereotypes, and the Alba reputation—all of them precepts associated with preserving the past by repeating it. Whatever mitigating effect her former husbands may have had on her dominance is removed with the death of her second husband, to whom the daughters can no longer turn for protection. As she warns Magdalena, "Ya no puedes ir con el cuento a tu padre" (63). Invoking Lacan and Kristeva, Blake has shown how Bernarda becomes "the maternal version of the father" ("Bernarda" 32). Absolute authority demands absolute obedience. In the manner of autocratic politicians who label modern media as "enemies of the people" and political rivals as "the enemy from within," any deviation from blind adherence to the norms set by Bernarda is enough to cast the offender as an enemy, even when that offender is an enemy from within—her own daughter, who "deja de ser hija para convertirse en una enemiga" (125). As Michael A. Gómez suggests, in imposing her will through the authority vested in her as the matriarch, Bernarda is enslaved by the mantle of tradition she takes on (229–30). At its core, however, that mantle is an empty shell, for it consists of demanding that her subjects abide by norms whose rationales she is at a loss to explain—after all, those norms were

[8] Obsessive cleanliness is another recurring theme. Given Bernarda's fanatical need for control, order, and cleanliness, a present-day therapist might well diagnose her with Obsessive-Compulsive Personality Disorder (OCPD). Some psychologists have observed that there is an "association between OCPD and rage, anger, hostility, and/or aggression," traits not found wanting in Bernarda (Jennifer Bartz et al. 327). Closer to Lorca's day, Sigmund Freud coined the term "housewife's psychosis" in his analysis of a mother who has no understanding of her offspring's interests and is "occupied all day long in cleaning the house," a chore Bernarda relegates to her servants (179).

conceived not by her but by an historical order that precedes her. Under her jurisdiction, traditions must be followed even if their original purpose is lost. The rote thinking and non-thinking she thereby promotes (recall her assertion, "No pienso ... Yo ordeno" [112]), applies even to superstitions. When Adela asks why Santa Barbara is invoked when lightning strikes, Bernarda replies, "Los antiguos sabían muchas cosas que hemos olvidado" (134).[9] The politician gives no justifications for the rules she imposes, beyond occasionally saying they are repetitions of what was done in the past. "The emptiness of the authoritarian superego is perceived by the authoritarian personality, but instead of formulating reflexive critique, this so-produced aggressive potential is directed towards lower social groups and outsiders" (Herzog). The "lower social groups" here explicitly consist of her servants and everyone in this rural community she considers beneath her. Like a cruel tyrant who has no compunctions about acting outside the law, Bernarda goads onlookers to kill the young woman who has had a child out of wedlock "antes que lleguen los guardias" (121). Not averse to violence, she brandishes a shotgun to shoot Pepe and strikes her daughters with her walking cane when they disobey (66, 108, 148). That cane, with which she often pounds the floor to demand attention, is tantamount to a scepter or phallic stick that symbolizes her authority and, as Brenda Logan Capuccio argues, her "new 'masculine' status" (39). When at last Adela frees herself from the politician's grip and breaks the symbol in two, declaring, "Esto hago yo con la vara de la dominadora," Bernarda quashes the rebellion as any autocrat would, by force, escalating from the symbolic power of the cane to the firepower of the shotgun (148).

In the climactic peripeteia and the pithy denouement of the closing scene, death, silence, decency, reputation, despotism, the force of nature, and gender stereotyping coalesce to produce a crescendo of doom. This previously overlooked thematic density, traceable throughout *La casa de Bernarda Alba* and culminating in the closing scene, speaks to the work's economy of invention and to the artfulness of Lorca's creative loom, which managed to produce a work that, in

---

[9] Bernarda is apparently unaware that, long before the advent of the lightning rod, the catholic church designated Santa Bárbara, patron saint of architects and fire fighters, as well as holy protector against storms and lightning.

spite of its copious repetitions, never seems repetitive. Qualifying each motif as denoting difference or repetition brings into prominence the political overtones of the despot's conduct, her subjugation methods, the taxonomy of cultural values she espouses, and the stultifying results of her efforts, as well as the underlying nature of the rebellious forces that threaten to topple her regime. What unfolds before us is an unevenly matched contest between a creative impulse that seeks to affirm difference and a dominant ideology that seeks to quash it and to perpetuate itself by enshrining and imposing the values of an antiquated patriarchal society. Bernarda governs by means of proclamation, intimidation, mass surveillance, sporadic violence, silencing opposition, favoring optics over facts, promoting rote thinking, and branding disloyal subjects as enemies, even if they are her own progeny. In all of these respects she mirrors the most salient features of a despotic politician who seeks to prolong their hegemony and to prevent any sign of difference from surfacing in their realm. Thus, even while closeted or disguised as a tragic family clash among women, the play represents not only a stinging condemnation of authoritarianism and the norms of bourgeois Spanish society, but also of what autocratic politicians seek to protect: their power, their reputations, and the status quo. The rebellious voice of the poet, represented by Adela, María Josefa, the force of nature, and, presumably, Lorca himself, calls for breathing life and difference into the morbid prison house of repetition patriarchal society has wrought. It calls for donning a green dress when all must wear black.[10] It calls for unbridled love to outwit an unnatural betrothal. And it calls for speaking truth to power, unmasking hypocrisies, and challenging mindless and outdated social norms.

As a free thinker living in a society steeped in tradition, Lorca knew too well the travails of breaking norms and being different. As a poet and playwright, he was well acquainted with the aesthetics of difference and repetition. In this tragedy, he draws on his mastery of that aesthetics to show us how a society that mandates repetition and

---

[10] An early sign of her rebelliousness and connection with nature's creative force, Adela models the dress before the chickens in the corral, later declaring she will wear it in public (73, 78). On connotations of the color green in Lorca's work, see Robert G. Havard (813–17).

rejects difference ultimately reaps disaster. Tragically, the forces that deny that which differs, as depicted in his final work, are of the same ilk as those that in August of 1936 cut short his life. His creation, Martirio, knows enough about life to assert that "las cosas se repiten. Y veo que todo es una terrible repetición" (71). The fatal consequence of that "terrible repetición" in *La casa de Bernarda Alba* is a clarion call to break the autocratic spell of mindless repetition, a call that is emblematic of the arts' celebration of difference in the early part of the twentieth century and that continues to resonate with audiences today.

WORKS CITED

Álvarez Castaño, Emilio José. "*Desire Under the Elms* y *La casa de Bernarda Alba*: Análisis comparado de dos dramas rurales." *Hipertexto*, vol. 17, 2013, pp. 88–99, www.utrgv.edu/hipertexto/en-us/all-issues/index.htm.

Arango, Manuel Antonio. *Símbolo y simbología en la obra de Federico García Lorca*. Fundamentos, 1995.

Badenes, José I. "All About Mothers: Sacred Violence in Federico García Lorca's *The House of Bernarda Alba* and Tennessee Williams's *Suddenly, Last Summer*." *Text & Presentation*, edited by Graley Herren, McFarland & Company, 2012, pp. 125–35.

Barrick, Mac E. "'Los antiguos sabían muchas cosas': Superstition in *La casa de Bernarda Alba*." *Hispanic Review*, vol. 48, no. 4, 1980, pp. 469–77.

Bartz, Jennifer, Alicia Kaplan, and Eric Hollander. "Obsessive-Compulsive Personality Disorder." *Personality Disorders: Toward the DSM-V*, edited by William O'Donohue, Katherine A. Fowler, and Scott O. Lilienfel, Sage Press, 2007, pp. 327–53.

Blake, Thomas. "Bernarda Alba and Frogs With No Tongues." *MP: An Online Feminist Journal*, vol. 3, no. 1, 2010, pp. 24–38, www.academinist.org/wp-content/uploads/2010/06/030103Blake_Frogs.pdf.

—. "Maternity, Morality, and Metaphor: Galdós's *Doña Perfecta*, Lorca's *The House of Bernarda Alba*, and Andalusian Culture." *Cognition, Literature, and History*, edited by Mark J. Bruhn and Donald R. Wehrs, Routledge, 2014, pp. 115–33.

Blum, Bilha. "'¡Silencio, he dicho!' Space, Language, and Characterization as Agents of Social Protest in Lorca's Rural Tragedies." *Reading Modern Drama*, edited by Alan Ackerman, U of Toronto P, 2012, pp. 46–61.

Cabello Pino, Manuel. "La influencia de *La casa de Bernarda Alba* en la creación de personajes femeninos en la obra de Gabriel García Márquez." *Bulletin of Hispanic Studies,* vol. 93, no. 2, 2016, pp. 209–20.

Capuccio, Brenda Logan. "Twisted Systems and Sisters: A Structuralist Analysis of *La casa de Bernarda Alba.*" *Hispanic Journal,* vol. 14, 1993, pp. 37–46.

Deleuze, Gilles. *Difference and Repetition,* translated by Paul Patton, Continuum, 2001.

Dokou, Christina. *Gendered Oracles: The Teiresian Androgyne in Sophocles, Eliot, Lorca, Ritsos,* 1997. Pennsylvania State U, PhD dissertation.

Doménech, Ricardo. "Símbolo, mito y rito en *La casa de Bernarda Alba.*" La casa de Bernarda Alba *y el teatro de García Lorca*, Cátedra, 1985, pp. 187–209.

Dougherty, Dru. "El lenguaje del silencio en el teatro de García Lorca." *Anales de la Literatura Española Contemporánea,* vol. 11, 1986, pp. 91–110.

Fernández Cifuentes, Luis. "García Lorca y el teatro convencional." *Iberoromania,* vol. 17, 1983, pp. 66–99.

Foucault, Michel. *Discipline and Punish: The Birth of the Prison,* translated by Alan Sheridan, Vintage, 1995.

Fox, Linda C. "Power in the Family and Beyond: Doña Perfecta and Bernarda Alba as Manipulators of Their Destinies." *Hispanófila,* vol. 29, 1985, pp. 57–65.

Freud, Sigmund. *The Freud Reader,* edited by Peter Gray, W. W. Norton, 1989.

Gabriele, John P. "Mapping the Boundaries of Gender: Men, Women and Space in *La casa de Bernarda Alba.*" *Hispanic Journal,* vol. 15, no. 2, 1994, pp. 381–92.

Galán Font, Eduardo. "La huella de *La Celestina* en *La casa de Bernarda Alba.*" *Revista de Literatura,* vol. 52, 1990, pp. 203–14.

García-Abad García, María Teresa. "Lorca/Spielberg: ¿La casa de Schindler o la lista de Bernarda?" *Boletín de la Fundación Federico García Lorca,* 1998, pp. 123–34.

García Lorca, Federico. *Bodas de sangre,* edited by Mario Hernández, Alianza, 1984.

—. *La casa de Bernarda Alba*, edited by Mario Hernández, Alianza, 1986.

—."La monja gitana." *Romancero gitano.* www.cervantesvirtual.com/obra-visor/romancero-gitano-785135/html/.

Godoy, Juan M. "The Voice from the Closet: The Articulation of Desire in *La casa de Bernarda Alba.*" *Pacific Coast Philology*, vol. 39, 2004, pp. 102–111.

Gómez, Michael A. "*La casa de Bernada Alba.* A Nietzschean Reading." *Bulletin of Hispanic Studies,* vol. 87, no. 2, 2010, pp. 221–39.

Havard, Robert G. "The Symbolic Ambivalence of *Green* in García Lorca and Dylan Thomas." *The Modern Language Review,* vol. 67, 1972, pp. 810–19.

Herzog, Benno. "Authoritarianism as Pathology of Recognition: The Sociological Substance and Actuality of the Authoritarian Personality." *Humanities and Social Sciences Communications* 8, 135 (2021). https://doi.org/10.1057/s41599-021-00819-5.

Levy, Michel Frucht. "Of Time and the River: Lorca's *La casa de Bernarda Alba* and Chekhov's *Try sestry.*" *La Chispa '85: Selected Proceedings*, edited by Gilbert Paolini, Tulane UP, 1985, pp. 203–12.

Lima, Robert. "Missing in Action: Invisible Males in *La casa de Bernarda Alba.*" *Bucknell Review,* vol. 45.1, 2001, pp. 136–47.

Poeta, Salvatore J. "Poetic and Social Patterns of Symmetry and Contrast in Lorca's *La casa de Bernarda Alba.*" *Hispania,* vol. 82, no. 4, 1999, pp. 740–49.

Radke, Helena R.M., Matthew J. Hornsey, Chris G. Sibley, and Fiona Kate Barlow. "Negotiating the Hierarchy: Social Dominance Orientation Among Women Is Associated with the Endorsement of Benevolent Sexism." *Australian Journal of Psychology*, vol. 70, 2, pp. 158-66.

Rice, Mary. "Gender and Authority in *La casa de Bernarda Alba* and *Escuadra hacia la muerte.*" *Entre actos: Diálogos sobre teatro español entre siglos,* edited by Martha T. Halsey and Phyllis Zatlin, Estreno, 1999, pp. 337–44.

Rosendofsky, Jaroslav. "Algunas observaciones sobre *Doña Perfecta* de B. Pérez Galdós y *La casa de Bernarda Alba* de F. García Lorca." *Etudes romanes de Brno,* vol. 114, 1966, pp. 181–200.

Urbina, Eduardo. "De Calderón a Lorca: El tema del honor en *La casa de Bernarda Alba.*" *Approaches to the Theater of Calderón*, edited by Michael D. McGaha, UP of America, 1982, pp. 259–70.

ENTREVISTAS

EMMA SEPÚLVEDA Y LA FICCIÓN DE LA REALIDAD

Por A. Mendoza

EMMA SEPÚLVEDA aparece en pantalla con una sonrisa luminosa que contrasta delicadamente con la firmeza de su mirada. Desde Valencia, donde actualmente reside, la escritora y activista argentino-estadounidense habla con un tono dulce pero decidido, una mezcla de calidez y convicción que sólo puede pertenecer a alguien que ha recorrido muchos territorios —geográficos, literarios y emocionales— y que ha salido fortalecida de cada uno de ellos.

A sus espaldas, la luz tenue del Mediterráneo acompaña nuestra conversación virtual. Yo, en el norte de México; ella, en la costa este de España. "Aquí me quiero quedar", dirá más adelante, describiendo la paz que encontró en esta ciudad tras una vida marcada por el exilio, la lucha social, la literatura y la denuncia constante.

Conversamos sobre su libro *Cuando mi cuerpo dejó de ser tu casa* (Memorias de Ilse en Colonia Dignidad), una novela de ficción basada en una historia tan real que duele. El testimonio de una niña-mujer atrapada en una secta alemana instalada en Chile, donde la obediencia era la ley y la represión, el pan de cada día. Con una voz narrativa construida desde la infancia, Emma logra dar cuenta de los horrores que vivieron —y que aún arrastran— muchas mujeres en ese entorno, mientras cuestiona, como siempre lo ha hecho, las estructuras de poder que lo permitieron.

Desde la crudeza del relato hasta la ternura como trinchera frente a la violencia, Sepúlveda hilvana temas como la migración, la maternidad impuesta, el papel de la memoria colectiva y el rol político de la literatura. La entrevista —lúcida, íntima, rabiosa por momentos— es también un reflejo de ese pulso vital que atraviesa su obra: la necesidad de contar lo que muchos prefieren olvidar.

Habla de Ilse, su protagonista, como si aún la acompañara. Y tal vez así sea. Después de todo, como ella misma dice: "Este libro me duele. La historia me duele". Pero también confiesa que escribirlo la liberó. Y que, como muchas de sus heroínas, Ilse logra no sólo sobrevivir, sino imaginar un futuro posible. Porque incluso en los peores infiernos, Emma Sepúlveda siempre encuentra una rendija por donde entra la luz.

Raíces, escritura y migración

A. Mendoza: Emma, tras haber vivido tantos años fuera de tu región natal, ¿dirías que tu obra reafirma tu identidad latinoamericana?

Emma Sepúlveda: Exacto. Y lo pienso porque tras haber vivido tantos años en Estados Unidos logré entender que no es el país acogedor que muchos imaginan. Es decir, aunque me nacionalicé, formé familia allá y también obtuve muchos reconocimientos a mi labor académica y activismo político, nunca lo sentí como casa. Mi corazón siempre estuvo en Chile, aunque nací en Argentina, donde estaba la familia de mi madre. Pero en Chile viví los años más formativos, doce años en el mismo colegio católico de mujeres. Ahí aprendí a escribir, a pensar, a resistir. Después, estudié cinco años de universidad en Chile, pero el golpe militar me obligó a salir tres meses antes de graduarme. Llegué a EE.UU. sin idioma, sin título, y con la certeza de que aquel país había jugado un rol clave en la destrucción de la democracia en Chile.

A. Mendoza: ¿Y cómo fue abrirte camino en ese nuevo contexto?

Emma Sepúlveda: Fue duro, pero encontré aliados en la comunidad migrante. Trabajé con exiliados, con centroamericanos, con mexicanos. Mi primer empleo fue en un restaurante mexicano. Curiosamente, al salir de Chile por tierra no me dejaron entrar a México; el país cerraba sus puertas ante el éxodo. Tuve que esperar un mes y medio en Guatemala sin éxito.

A. Mendoza: Ironías que aún nos tocan. La migración sigue siendo un campo de batalla política y humana.

Emma Sepúlveda: Exactamente. Aun así, amo México. Años después volví como profesora invitada. Pero en EE.UU., además de migrante, me convertí en mujer de color. En Chile era blanca. Ese cambio forzado de identidad me marcó. Luego, trabajar en la campaña de Obama me abrió otra perspectiva. Él me nombró en la comisión Fulbright, uno de los mayores honores que he tenido. Sin embargo, cuando llegó Trump, supe que tenía que partir otra vez.

A. Mendoza: ¿Y fue entonces cuando decidiste mudarte a Valencia?

Emma Sepúlveda: Sí. Después de casi 50 años lejos de Chile, aunque iba seguido, decidimos ir a España. Valencia me cautivó. Caminando por sus parques sentí: aquí quiero morir. Vendimos todo en EE.UU. y Chile, y empezamos de nuevo. Aquí hay paz, no hay miedo. No temo ser atacada por ser extranjera. Ha sido una liberación. Y aunque Estados Unidos me dio mucho, yo creo que el sueño americano lo mantenemos vivo los migrantes. El pueblo estadounidense, en cambio, ha perdido la esperanza. Por eso es tan fácil que figuras como Trump los engañen. Pero yo me siento orgullosa de haber aportado mi grano de arena para cambiar algunas cosas.

La otra cara de la migración: colonos y destrucción

A. Mendoza: En tu libro, abordas una migración muy distinta a la que suele retratarse: una comunidad blanca, alemana, con privilegios, y un exilio por demás oscuro que se instala con apoyo del gobierno chileno. Una historia que obliga a replantearnos cómo América Latina ha recibido a ciertos migrantes, contraria a la narrativa actual que solo muestra la migración desde una perspectiva sesgada.

Emma Sepúlveda: Fíjate que tú eres la primera persona que toca ese tema. Nunca nadie había notado el privilegio de estos colonos solo por venir de la Europa blanca. Si hubieran venido de África, probablemente ni siquiera los dejaban entrar. Se trata de una migración profundamente marcada por el racismo y la complicidad institucional. Y es un tema que se omite al hablar de lo que implica realmente migrar a un país como Chile en ese entonces. Sinceramente un tema que se deja de lado al pensar, sobre todo, en la narrativa de la migración en la "América" blanca.

La narradora y el punto de vista de la novela

A. Mendoza: Elegiste una voz narrativa infantil. Es probable que la niñez sea el proceso más difícil y el más profundo y sin embargo uno de los más obviados cuando se habla de temas como el que tratas en tu libro. ¿Cómo llegaste a esa decisión tan poderosa?

Emma Sepúlveda: Fue muy difícil encontrar esa voz, pero una vez que la encontré, todo fluyó. Me ayudó un encuentro con una mujer en la colonia, vestida aún con uniforme antiguo, que me habló como una niña, una mujer-niña. Con mucha dificultad para expresarse debido al trauma y a la escasa educación que les permitieron en la colonia, me dijo que estaba mal, pero que estaba mejor cuando Paul Schäfer vivía. Esa contradicción, esa mente atrapada, fue clave. Nunca aprendieron realmente. No sabían leer, no conocían el mundo. Incluso me contaron que muchas se casaron sin mantener intimidad con sus parejas, un tema por demás tabú como tantos otros y estaban sorprendidas de no saber por qué no quedaban embarazadas. Vivieron aisladas, sin entender su propio cuerpo. Eso me ayudó a crear a Ilse: una mujer-niña que no pudo crecer en libertad pero que logra reconstruirse y liberarse.

Maternidades y opresión

A. Mendoza: Mientras la sexualidad libre es reprimida en dicho contexto, curiosamente la maternidad aparece como una herramienta de control más que como un derecho. ¿Cómo desarrollaste esa dimensión tan cruda del relato?

Emma Sepúlveda: En mi novela, narré lo terrible que es que algunas mujeres terminen siendo enemigas de otras mujeres al seguir líderes patriarcales. Pasa en la vida real: muchas mujeres no votaron por Harris, prefirieron a un hombre como Trump, que odia a las mujeres y las ha violentado abiertamente. En la novela, eso está presente. Las madres cumplen un rol impuesto y doloroso para servir a sus líderes quienes las violentan a pesar de necesitarlas. Algo demasiado actual si recordamos al actual vicepresidente de EE.UU. que llamó 'cat ladies' a las mujeres sin hijos, con ese desprecio hacia quienes no cumplen el rol tradicional porque no les sirven en su programa ideológico. Es una violencia simbólica tan profunda como la física.

Figuras femeninas, resistencia y escritura

A. Mendoza: Ilse escribe. Y al hacerlo, se libera. ¿Buscaste hacer de la escritura una forma de resistencia simbólica?

Emma Sepúlveda: Siempre he querido dar a las víctimas herramientas para desvictimizarse. Ilse representa esa posibilidad: encontrar su libertad en medio del infierno. No solo escapa físicamente, también logra sacar la secta de dentro de sí. Su amiga Angélica no pudo hacerlo. Muchas volvieron. Muchas siguen atrapadas. Pero Ilse cree en la vida, en el amor, incluso después de haber perdido la capacidad de tener hijos. Me inspiré en una pareja real que vive en el sur de Chile, dos sobrevivientes sin una gota de odio. Ellos me dieron esperanza para construir personajes con dignidad, incluso después del trauma.

También me ocurrió con las mujeres del accidente de los 33 mineros. Pasé un mes en el campamento. Vi una fuerza en ellas que rara vez se reconoce. Y lo digo convencida: la resiliencia de muchas mujeres supera la de los hombres.

Literatura, periodismo y denuncia social

A. Mendoza: En contextos donde el periodismo falla, la literatura ilumina lo que otros callan. Tu libro es un ejemplo claro de eso.

Emma Sepúlveda: Con la pluma se pueden provocar cambios. Este libro fue el que más me exigió en términos de investigación. Conocí la historia de Colonia Dignidad desde muy joven. Leí sobre Wolfgang Müller, un muchacho que escapó. Y luego supe de una mujer que dejó a sus hijos al intentar huir. Me obsesioné. Incluso lo propuse como tema de doctorado, pero me dijeron que era historia, no literatura.

Cuando la editorial me pidió hacer un libro de no ficción, les dije que no. Yo quería contar lo que no se había dicho: la historia de las mujeres. Leí todo. Archivos, artículos, libros. Tengo cajas de material. Y lo más duro es que casi todo es real. La ficción es mínima. Ilse está basada en una niña real. Lo mínimo es ficción.

A. Mendoza: Y eso es lo más potente del libro. Que logra conmover desde la verdad, sin necesidad de disfrazarla.

Emma Sepúlveda: Por eso al final digo que esta es la ficción de la realidad y la realidad de la ficción.

El valor del libro y las voces latinoamericanas

A. Mendoza: ¿Cómo viviste emocionalmente este proceso, sabiendo que estabas trabajando con verdades tan duras?

Emma Sepúlveda: Fue agotador. Lo escribí en pandemia. No podía dormir muchas noches. Lo que relataba era real, era brutal. Y aún ahora, cada vez que presento el libro, me duele. Pero también me alegra ver que está siendo leído y reconocido.

A. Mendoza: Y además, el libro sigue creciendo. Ahora llega a nuevos lectores fuera de América Latina.

Emma Sepúlveda: Sí. En 2024 se tradujo al alemán. Era un sueño. Lo presenté en la Feria del Libro de Frankfurt, invitada por el gobierno chileno. Ahora esperamos la versión en inglés. También ya terminamos el guion para la película. Estoy segura de que esta historia aún tiene mucho que decir. Estamos en un momento crítico. Las mujeres estamos perdiendo derechos. Que este libro se lea, se vea, se hable... es urgente.

A. Mendoza: Gracias, Emma, por tu tiempo, por tu voz, y por darle vida a una historia tan necesaria. Tu libro deja huella, como todo lo que toca la verdad.

AUTORES

Tino Villanueva writes in Spanish and English to explore memory, longing, and history. His books include *So Spoke Penelope* and *Scene from the Movie GIANT* a 1994 American Book Award winner. Founder of Imagine Publishers, Villanueva has edited Chicano poetry journals and anthologies and taught at Wellesley College and Boston University. He lives in Boston. His poetry collections include *Hay Otra Voz Poems* (1972), *Shaking Off the Dark* (1984), *Crónica de mis años peores* (1987), *Chronicle of My Worst Years* (1994), *Primera Causa / First Cause* (1999), *Il canto del cronista: Antologia poetica* (2002), among others.

Vitoria Pérez es poeta del estado de Luisiana. Fascinada por la tecnología obsoleta, su poesía se abarca temas de luchas de liberación, comunicación manual–digital y dolor crónico corporal–mental. Su poesía ha sido incluida en *Déraciné*, *Réapparition*, *Small World City*, *Expanded Field*, y en otros lares literarios.

Enriqueta Ochoa (1928–2008) fue una poeta mexicana nacida en Torreón, Coahuila. Educada en casa, desde joven se formó en lenguas, música y literatura clásica. Su poesía, de raíz mística y profundamente íntima, explora temas como la vida, la muerte y el "femenino sagrado". Autora de obras como *El retorno de Electra* y *Bajo el oro de los pequeños trigos*, también fundó la revista *Hierba* y enseñó literatura en varias universidades mexicanas. Recibió reconocimientos como la Placa de Oro de Coahuila y la Medalla de Oro Bellas Artes. Su legado sigue vivo en el Concurso Nacional de Poesía que lleva su nombre.

J. J. Steinfeld is a Canadian poet, fiction writer, and playwright living on Prince Edward Island (Epekwitk), where he is patiently waiting for Godot's arrival and a phone call from Kafka. While waiting, he has published 25 books, including *An Unauthorized Biography of Being* (Stories, Ekstasis Editions, 2016), *Absurdity, Woe Is Me, Glory Be* (Poetry, Guernica Editions, 2017), *A Visit to the Kafka Café* (Poetry, Ekstasis Editions, 2018), *Gregor Samsa Was Never in The Beatles* (Stories, Ekstasis Editions, 2019), *Morning Bafflement and Timeless Puzzlement* (Poetry, Ekstasis Editions, 2020), *Somewhat Absurd, Somehow Existential* (Poetry, Guernica Editions, 2021), *Acting on the Island* (Stories, Pottersfield Press, 2022), *As You Continue to Wait* (Poetry, Ekstasis Editions, 2022), and *My Post-Holocaust Second*

Generation Voice: History / Memory / Identity (Poetry, Ekstasis Editions, 2025).

Lyn Good (they/them) is a Minnesota-based writer specializing in lyric poetry. They're on a constant journey to find their voice, and their foremost mission in life is shattering the boundary between their dreaming self and their self that experiences what some might call "reality." They can also be found in the wild writing and performing in plays.

Richard Oyama's poems, stories and essays have appeared in *Premonitions: The Kaya Anthology of New Asian North American Poetry*, *The Nuyorasian Anthology*, *Breaking Silence*, *Dissident Song*, *A Gift of Tongues*, *About Place*, *Konch Magazine*, *Pirene's Fountain*, *Tribes*, *Malpaís Review*, *Anak Sastra*, *Buddhist Poetry Review* and other literary journals. *The Country They Know* (Neuma Books 2005) is his first collection of poetry. He has a M.A. in English: Creative Writing from San Francisco State University. Currently retired, Oyama taught at California College of Arts in Oakland, University of California at Berkeley and University of New Mexico. His first novel in a trilogy, *A Riot Goin' On*, is forthcoming. He is currently at work on a young adult novel and a full-length poetry collection.

Majo Delgadillo is a graduate of the MFA in Creative Writing at the University of California, San Diego and the PhD program in Creative Writing in Spanish at the University of Houston, where she also was Student Artist-in-Residence in Neuroaesthetics at the IUCRC BRAIN Center. She writes about bodies, memory, pop culture, the fantastic, history, and horror, and is interested in how these interact and intersect. Her work has been published in *Carte Blanche Magazine*, *Camas Magazine*, the *Revista de la Universidad* and *Erizo Journal for the Arts*, among others. She has published the digital piece machine3.xyz and the book of short stories *Lullabies for the End of the World* (Bakstenen Huis, 2021) and its Spanish translation *Canciones de cuna para el fin del mundo* (Editorial Paraíso Perdido 2022). She was a finalist for the Casa Wabi Narrative Prize-Dharma Books 2023. She currently teaches at James Madison University in Virginia, USA.

Ryan Kulcak is a graduate student at the University of New Mexico currently residing in Houston, TX. When not writing or studying

Colonial Latin American History he works as a tutor of most subjects K-12. He is passionate about education, creation, and staying active in the addiction recovery community.

Blake Sanz won the Iowa Short Fiction Award for his collection of fiction, *The Boundaries of Their Dwelling*. His prose has appeared or is forthcoming in *The Georgia Review*, *Ecotone*, *The Missouri Review*, *American Short Fiction*, and elsewhere. A recipient of fellowships and conferences from Sewanee Writers Conference, Bread Loaf Writers' Conference, the Sozopol Fiction Seminars, and Napa Valley Writers' Conference, he teaches in the MFA program at the University of Wyoming.

Anjanette Delgado (Santurce, 1967) escribe sobre desamor, desarraigo y justicia social. Ganadora de un premio Emmy por periodismo de interés humano, es autora de las novelas: *La píldora del mal amor* (Atria, 2008) y *La clarividente de la Calle Ocho* (Penguin Random House, 2014). Ha escrito poesía, ficción y ensayos para el *New York Times* (Modern Love; Opinión), *NPR*, *Kenyon Review*, *Prairie Schooner*, Hostos Review (CUNY) y Tupelo Quarterly, entre otros. Editó la antología *Home in Florida: Latinx Writers and the Literature of Uprootedness* (University of Florida Press, 2021), Medalla de Oro por ficción colectiva en los Latino International Book Awards 2022. Anjanette se graduó en comunicaciones de la Universidad de Puerto Rico, Recinto de Río Piedras y posee una maestría en escritura creativa de la Universidad Internacional de la Florida.
www.anjanettedelgado.com

Judah Mahay is an Alaskan SFF author who revels in subverting genre into the literary by taking science to plausible extreme or threading magic into reality. His short work has been published in *Pinky Thinker Press*, *Harrisburg Magazine*, and others. Mahay was the first fiction author accepted to Robert Wilson's internationally acclaimed arts laboratory, The Watermill Center. In service of that venture, he was awarded a New York Foundation for the Arts grant. His professional memberships include Science Fiction & Fantasy Writers of America and the Alaska Writers Guild. Academically, he earned his MFA in Literature & Creative Writing from Stony Brook Southampton. Mahay teaches as an English Professor at Penn State University and

Millersville University, while in the summer, he teaches gifted youth at Johns Hopkins Center for Talented Youth.

Zach Keali'i Murphy is a Hawaii-born writer with a background in cinema. His stories appear in *The MacGuffin*, *Reed Magazine*, *The Coachella Review*, *Lunch Ticket*, *Raritan Quarterly*, *Another Chicago Magazine*, *Little Patuxent Review*, *Flash Frog*, and more. He has published the chapbook *Tiny Universes* (Selcouth Station Press). He lives with his wonderful wife, Kelly, in St. Paul, Minnesota.

Daniel Snyder is a writer with dozens of essays and stories published in magazines and journals. He plays the accordion quite well, and the piano and guitar quite badly, which is fine because he never wanted to be a Rock Star. All he's ever wanted is for people to read his work. He and his wife currently live in South Carolina.

Olga Isabel Castilla Rocha, nacida el 4 de julio del 2002. Estudiante de la Universidad del Norte de Barranquilla, Colombia, en el pregrado de Lenguas Modernas y Cultura. Una de las ganadoras del Concurso Nacional de Cuento de Colombia en el año 2021. Inclinada a la escritura creativa de distintos géneros narrativos y líricos, especialmente de cuentos y poemas. Amante de escritores asiáticos, como Haruki Murakami, Mieko Kawakami y Han-Kang. Fiel seguidora de creaciones literarias de escritoras latinoamericanas como Marvel Moreno y Piedad Bonnett.

Wifredo de Ràfols is Graduate Director of the Spanish Graduate Program at the University of Nevada, Reno. He received his MA in English from the Johns Hopkins University and PhD in Spanish from the University of California, Davis. He teaches a wide variety of courses in Spanish literature, culture, and literary theory. His publications examine works by Zorrilla, Galdós, Valle-Inclán, Eugene O'Neill, Juan Ramón Jiménez, Jorge Guillén, and Federico García Lorca. His general research interests include hermeneutics, artificial reading, and bias studies.

Emma Sepúlveda es poeta, narradora, ensayista, fotógrafa y activista. Nacida en Argentina y criada en Chile, emigró a Estados Unidos en 1974, donde obtuvo un doctorado en literatura española en la Universidad de California, Davis. Fundadora del *Latino Research*

Center en la Universidad de Nevada, Reno, y la primera latina en postularse al Senado de Nevada, su obra literaria aborda temas de migración, política y memoria. Ha publicado más de treinta libros y ha sido reconocida nacional e internacionalmente. Actualmente es *Foundation Professor Emerita* en la Universidad de Nevada, Reno.

Contributors Across Issues

Cristina Rivera Garza • Tino Villanueva • Gabriela Alemán • Regina Rheda • Pedro Ángel Palou • José Prats Sariol • Saúl Cuevas • Guillermo Corral • Sarah Rafael García • Daniel Herrera • Judith Castañeda Suarí • Lucía Baskaran • María Cañas • Mario Martz • Hisham Bustani • Susana Chávez-Silverman • Lupita Eyde-Tucker • Felipe Lomelí • José Manuel Ortiz Soto • Consuelo Hernández • Ewa Mazierska • Harold Alvarado Tenorio • Ilana Luna • Jorge Manzanilla • Sebastian Ocampos • Eunice Adorno • Francisco Álvarez Koki • Natalia Chamorro • John Madera • Lucía Orellana • Sebastian Ocampos • Rodrigo Toscano • Francisco Díaz Klassen • J. J. Steinfeld.

PAGE INTENTIONALLY LEFT BLANK

DIGITUS INDIE PUBLISHERS
www.digitusindie.com
EDITORES INDEPENDIENTES

www.ingramcontent.com/pod-product-compliance
Lightning Source LLC
Chambersburg PA
CBHW061104100726
47911CB00012B/388

* 9 7 8 0 9 9 8 2 5 3 9 8 5 *